Wiz

Duos

Book 3

Wiz Duos

Book 3

Ruthanna Emrys & Andrew Knighton

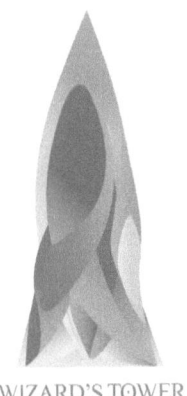

WIZARD'S TOWER

Wizard's Tower Press

Rhydaman, Cymru

Wiz Duos

Book 3

Stories by Ruthanna Emrys & Andrew Knighton

Edited by Roz Clarke & Joanne Hall

Cover art by Roz Clarke
Cover design by Ben Baldwin

Book design by Cheryl Morgan

First published by Wizard's Tower Press,
October 2025

ISBN: 978-1-917950-23-7

http://wizardstowerpress.com/

Contents

FOREWORD

By
Roz Clarke & Joanne Hall

Welcome to another Wiz Duo – the third in our new series and the first one to feature stories from open submissions. We're absolutely delighted to bring you these stories from Ruthanna Emrys and Andrew Knighton.

The stories share the themes of landscape and the magic that can be found in the familiar and the homely, and the friendships that can become found family. Both explore the ways in which people and places are sources both of grief and conflict, and the comfort we can find. In very different ways, they both tackle themes of freedom and control, how the open hand and the open way can bind us in community when those with power seek to parcel up land and lives for sale.

Ruthanna's story is an uplifting adventure in which a diverse group of friends finds they've bought a house with a history, and a set of obligations that start with hospitality to a teenager betrayed by her parents, and eventually throw them into conflict with an ancient power of the land.

In Andrew's poignant, moving tale, a young man returns to the home of his teenage years, and, through attempting to reconnect with lost friends, discovers that he must use his connection to the land to protect it from ruination.

It's difficult to say much more about the delicious way these stories complement one another without spoiling the plots, so we'll just say that as soon as we had read them both we could see that they were a perfect fit for each other, and for the Wiz Duos format, and we hope you will enjoy them as much as we did.

The Sheltering Flame

Ruthanna Emrys

THE SHELTERING FLAME

For everyone who still opens their door to strangers,
and for everyone who's knocked and
gotten the help they needed.

RUTHANNA EMRYS

THE SHELTERING FLAME

The house isn't haunted, exactly. It is, I'm starting to think, awake. It was cheap, anyway, a half-fixed fixer-upper with its pedigree lost to a town records fire several decades ago, its more recent history a mess of zoning violations, informal frathouse property damage, and sketchy medical offices.

Ours, now.

We are also sketchy: three college friends who fantasized about starting an intentional community together before we surrendered to the sacrifices demanded by academia. Del, who tried to make a commuting marriage work for a decade, stuttering along the tenure track at a tiny ag school in upstate New York before losing both the marriage and the tenure review—who called me at 2am having given up on love, gender, and teaching, but not art, and with no idea what to do next. Candace, who jumped from yearly contract to yearly contract, spiraling down the dead end of adjunct teaching until she decided it was saner and more profitable to be an unemployed folklorist. And me. I'm the success story of the lot—the one who slid helplessly and thoughtlessly all the way to my tenure offer at an esteemed psych department, only to realize that my chronic nausea stemmed from the simple fact that I hated my job. That I was only really happy working with my hands, fixing up the shitty little house I'd been able to sort-of-afford on an assistant professor's salary.

And here we all are, together again in a crumbling, right-angle-free Victorian on a back road outside Amherst. The mountain views are gorgeous, the land is affordable, and the economy is non-existent.

We've gotten some insulation into the walls, fixed the windowpanes that were actually broken, and varnished the floors with the ridiculous stuff meant for sailboats that

Candace's family gifted us. It still stinks, though bearably with windows open to the late-summer breeze. A whiff of chemical solidity, another sacrifice. This afternoon I'm making my way through the doorknobs. Doorknobs are simple, but Del got stuck in their bedroom last night, and we spent a stupid half-hour trying various tricks with wires and credit cards before we got them free. This morning they threatened to route treehouse-style rope ladders out of their window and over the still-rickety porch roof, so: doorknobs. Brass, because it's pretty and antibacterial and the local construction surplus co-op had a set of a dozen for two bucks each. Ropelike designs circle each one, naval loops and knots enticing the hand that grasps.

I unscrew the old knob from the door to my attic bedroom, work the rusty latch bolt out of its slot. The house complains and tugs against me, like when I try to comb a nasty tangle out of my niece's hair. I still don't know what to make of these moments, aside from the probability that my hold on reality is growing iffy. Clinical psych's not my area, but I figure that as long as your delusions don't encourage anything maladaptive, you may as well live with them. I pet the doorframe, like I would a nervous dog, and the feeling subsides.

I get the new knob in place, check that the mechanism actually works and that turning the handle consistently turns the bolt, and someone knocks on our front door.

"What the hell?" We don't know anyone here—all our friends from school have moved away, because see economy, and we haven't had the chance to introduce ourselves to the neighbors yet, let alone find out exactly how old our once-favorite queer bookshop makes us feel these days.

I start downstairs, and Del pokes their head out from their bedroom. "Are you getting that, Leah? If it's door-to-door religious salesmen, holler and I won't put on clothes."

I roll my eyes. "If it's door-to-door religious sales-kids, we let them in and feed them and show them that we're not

12

terrifying monsters. And if it's, like, an actual terrifying monster, I'd rather you already had clothes on."

Del comes out, revealing that they are, in fact, wearing a really excellent tunic printed with spiraling words: EVERY TIME YOU GET DRESSED REMEMBER, IF YOU DIE, THAT'S YOUR GHOST OUTFIT FOREVER. They've also dyed their buzz-cut hair with leopard print, something I didn't even know you could do at home. But I'm not surprised: I was there for Del's getting-my-PhD celebration concert where the girl in front of us had that dye job, have heard them swear often enough to do the same just as soon as tenure obviated the need for professionalism. "You look fabulous, and the vampire at the door better think so too."

The knock comes again. We troop downstairs and find Candace already there, turning to raise a practiced eyebrow before opening the door.

The kid clinging to the knocker isn't selling religion. Girl scout cookies, maybe—she looks like a younger-every-year freshman at best, the kind taking a deep breath before begging for a much-needed extension, the kind that wait until semester's end before admitting to poorly-treated depression, or sick kids, or whatever they've always been told is a terrible excuse for skin-of-the-teeth work. This one—white, lapis-haired, decked in jeans and an ill-fitting leather jacket—stares wide-eyed and takes that breath, then blurts out: "I'm Chloe Davis and I beg the protection of the house!"

This is not an entirely unfamiliar situation. It's weirder here than in an office with a big rainbow Safe Space sign on the door, but we've been taking in strays since the injured flying squirrel we rehabbed in my sophomore dorm room; even during plague years, when guests were forbidden, we all volunteered for hotlines or comforted students remotely or, in Candace's case, hosted one who couldn't safely go home. Reflex takes over. Candace pulls her inside, checking behind for unwanted exes or parents (none visible), and I bring out tea and soda and leftover banana bread, and Del sits the kid at the dining room table and asks, "What do you need?"

Chloe sniffs, obviously trying to hold back tears, and repeats, miserably, "The protection of the house. Please."

It seems weirdly formal—but I can also feel, real or not, the house perking up around me. "We offer the house's protection," I say slowly, not sure where the words spring from beyond my own varnish-addled imagination, "as you join in providing it."

Chloe gasps, whimpering not like she hates the response but like she didn't really expect it, and asks in a small voice, "What terms?"

"Suppose you start by telling us who you're hiding from?" suggests Candace. "And why you came *here*?"

The kid's eyes widen, and I can see her taking in the piles of still-packed boxes, the paint cans, tools lying under the window. She whimpers again. "You're not the keepers of the hearth."

My gaze darts to the fireplace dominating the end of the room, brickwork repair a project still to come. It's probably not what she means. "We're the people who bought the house," I offer. Apologetically: "There aren't a lot of good records of what it was before we bought it from the bank. It's been empty for a while."

"Oh, fuck capitalism!" she exclaims, and I shrug and say, "With you there."

Candace, ever practical, prods. "But you need help?"

"From the keepers of the hearth. If you don't know what you've got, how do I even know the house still works?"

That sense again, stronger, of something waking and eager for work. "I can feel it," I say slowly. *Is that maladaptive?* Candace's eyes narrow, but neither she nor Del acts like I'm being completely absurd. I trust the feeling, even if I shouldn't. I've had my hands in the house's guts and bones, architecturally intimate. "But I don't know what I'm feeling. Why don't you tell us?"

Chloe sighs theatrically, the trailing remnant of a teen-ager's conviction that all adults are stupid. "It's magic. You understand magic?"

Candace shrugs and says, "I'm Neopagan."

"I'm an atheist," says Del. "But I like rituals."

She can see my Magen David nose stud just fine, so all I say is, "The world's a weird place."

The kid rolls her eyes. "Not magic like religion. Magic like—okay, there are two kinds. The older kind is magic you do with yourself or a community. You say what you are, what you want, where your boundaries are, and you convince the universe to believe it. Like drawing bison and berry bushes on a cave wall, and becoming the people who provide for your tribe through the winter. Or you can define those things for something else—not another human, they've got their own selves—and it wakes up to be that thing."

I'm not sure if I believe her, or rather I'm not sure I'm willing to admit that I believe, but I say, "Like the house?"

She nods, eyes still narrow with suspicion. She takes a bite of banana bread and chews thoughtfully. "Sometime in the 1800s, the first keepers of the hearth made this place a haven, probably for the Underground Railroad. All the workers in the Valley know it's here, even if they don't use it much any more. The keepers have to offer hospitality to anyone who asks. And once you accept the house's hospitality, no one can hurt you or insult you or make you leave against your will, as long as you follow those rules for everyone else."

"Wait," says Del. "You're saying we have to let *anyone* into the house."

Candace snorts. "I *heard* you two. You were arguing about whether to welcome wandering missionaries naked or fully dressed."

"What if we don't?" persisted Del. "What if my ex shows up and I tell him to get lost because I don't feel like arguing about whether my art is too commercial?"

Chloe sighs dramatically. "I don't know. This is literally something my parents explained when I was ten and they were running through safety drills. I assume turning some-one away would either make the house into a supernatural-ly-useless stack of rooms, or just make it easier for a bank to repossess your ass. But if your ex insults your art, that's a violation of hospitality and you can do whatever you like after that."

Candace gets up and locks the door, demonstrating a distinct lack of faith in supernatural protection. "You still haven't answered my question. What are we protecting you from?"

She sighs again. "My parents."

"Okay," I say; this part, at least, I know. Kids sobbing in my office because coming out hit the limits of parental under-standing, or because those limits were broken long ago and they're just now realizing that other options exist. Or kids trying to pretend everything is fine and breaking slowly under loving pressure to do more, do better, color inside the right lines. "Want to tell us about it?"

Chloe hunches small. "Actually, it's not exactly... So the other kind of magic, the newer kind, is the magic of bargains. And that can be good, learning to be all diplomatic and live with other people and not-exactly-people, and you can get things done that way that you can't just by knowing your-self—but bargaining can also be as fucked-up as late-stage capitalism."

"Dealing with demons," Del suggests, sounding more like they're playing along than believing—or like they're trying to sound like that. When *do* we start taking the magic part seriously, and how does that look different from just taking seriously the worried kid flinging herself on our doorstep?

"I guess? None of the things that make deals are actually a great fit for the names humans put on them. But—I don't think it's that I was dating girls, you know. They'd've been fine if I'd just found girls they approved of, people who were

16

part of their world and understood the way they do things. But workers, magicians, are kind of a small group, and it gets incestuous pretty fast, so I was just—dating. It felt out of control to them, and they don't like feeling out of control. And then I had a bad breakup, and I guess it really freaked them out and they were afraid I'd get hurt again."

"So they did what?" I ask. Magic to make the universe listen to your own ideas about your identity, your own desires, doesn't sound ideal for controlling other people. She'd said you *couldn't* control other people's identities. *Who does it make me, how do I have to think, if I'm the sort of person who takes this seriously?*

"So they went up to the Notch," says Chloe, and right away I know this is going to be bad. Because every time I've driven by the old mining cut at the top of the mountain, I've felt like something was chasing me, maybe even trying to force me off the road. And for the ten minutes that it takes to drive through, I've *always* believed in magic.

"They made a deal and set me up with something for which the closest wrong word is 'succubus' or maybe 'faerie.' Inhumanly hot, and once you've been with them you won't want anything else, ever. And I can't believe my *parents* would even think of that, but I guess they decided it's safer and more predictable than just dealing with the hot mess of other humans, and if they set the terms then I'd have someone who could never run out on me."

"That sounds kind of terrifying." I can't think of anything else to say.

"Yeah. I felt pretty miserable about Addison, and I probably said something stupid and dramatic, but I'd rather go through that a thousand times than be safe with someone where neither of us has the choice to leave."

Candace stretches. "So what have you done with them so far?"

"Candace!" I do *not* want to hear about teenage succubus shenanigans; but if this is real (I need to stop that, I keep saying "if" but *something* real is happening) I probably do need to hear.

Chloe straightens and glares, and I like her particularly in this moment, that she goes for defiance where I'd hunch over in shame or embarrassment. "There was a stranger at the table at breakfast, and my parents told them 'now you kiss her,' and I ran out and kept going till I saw a bus, and then stayed on buses till I thought of this place and found the nearest stop and started walking, and I came here. I don't *want* to get all my hormones pulled sideways like a giant magnet! I want to date pretty girls who're embarrassed to have acne on their backs, and who wake up with their hair all messy, and who say stupid things when they're turned on, and who talk about anime or weird-ass cheeses or football! And who—" She runs up against the end of her words in a hiccupping sob, as imperfect and un-cinematic as the girl of her dreams.

I give her an awkward hug. "Let's figure out where the air mattress got packed and find a spare toothbrush, and we can sort the details out after."

Feelings are squishy and hard to deal with. Possibly-delu-sional occult systems raise an overwhelming set of questions about the nature of the universe, and whether I'm still basi-cally on the side of empirical evidence even if I'm no longer gathering it professionally. But logistics, solving problems you can touch, that's safe. I can patch roofs that keep out wind and fascists; I can gather food and pour drinks and tuck in blankets. I can make a warm place in a cold world, and invite people in. That's all that makes sense right now, and really, most of what's ever made sense.

Candace heads for her room to dig out the air mattress from wherever she stashed it after we got her a bed. I go to look for spare toothbrushes, which are probably in a box that is probably in one of the bathrooms (this house has an absurd number of bathrooms, clearly added somewhere in the late 20th century by someone who never wanted to wait in the hall for a shower, ever).

Del catches up with me on the second floor. "What is happening?"

I shrug, elbow-deep in a box of washcloths and miscellaneous half-full organic toothpaste tubes. "Kid's parents are screwed up. Trying to force her into a relationship she doesn't want, and she's scared. Beyond that, if you're asking me what to believe, I don't know."

"I'm up for not knowing and playing it by ear. I haven't known what world I was in since the divorce, and you're the one who convinced me to be okay taking my time to figure it out. This is just more of the same." They kneel to tear open another box, finding it full of tessellated gift soaps that I've been dragging across state lines, never using, for over a decade. "I'm asking what *you* believe. You look pretty upset, and I know you suck at taking your own advice."

I sigh, sitting back on my heels. "It's not even the not-knowing, honestly. It's the... not knowing how to know. I'm a scientist, or I was, and I have no idea what it says that I mostly *do* believe her. Weird intuitions about the house don't meet any reasonable evidentiary standard. I worry that I'm going to turn into an, an architecture whisperer." I sniff hard, dig fingers into my jeans so I won't have an entirely irrational breakdown that this is absolutely not the time for.

"What's wrong with being an Architecture Whisperer?" asks Del, making it sound like the tagline to a reality show.

"You tell me." I hug my arms, hunching in exactly the way Chloe didn't. "Am I still someone whose advice you care about, if I'm also the sort of person who thinks she can tell what a house is feeling?"

Del rolls their eyes and scoots over to hug me. "I don't love you for your evidentiary standards, you know. *You* like protecting people. If this turns out to be a giant prank or a kid with her reality tunnel turned inside out, we'll deal with it. And if it turns out that the world isn't what we thought it was, we'll deal with that too." After a moment they add. "I do believe at least part of it is true, though. If you describe yourself clearly enough, the world has to listen. It doesn't have to be nice about it, but it has to let you be yourself."

That's the part—I don't say—that I'm afraid of. Because it would mean that my whole life has been so roundabout because I *haven't* been clear enough. Or maybe I've just been wrong about who I was. Maybe I still am.

#

Back downstairs, Candace is grilling Chloe about fairy tale tropes. "So if your parents made a deal, is there some way out? Conditions that have to be met, or a price that can be paid? Pull you from a horse at midnight on Halloween? Give the succubus-thing a cloak? Gather an unlikely number of gems in an unlikely amount of time?"

"I don't *know*!" Chloe breaks in. "Mom didn't exactly give me the receipt! She didn't even introduce us."

Candace snaps her fingers. "What if we guess its name?"

"I have no fucking idea, but I think it probably would've come up if I stuck around long enough to get kissed, so probably not."

"Candace, slow down," Del suggests. "I know it's not every day that applied folklore turns out to be a practical field, but I think Chloe would tell us if there were an easy way out, no grilling required."

"I'm sorry," says Chloe. "I don't know enough about this stuff, because my parents always told me it was too dangerous. Fine for them, apparently. And I'm furious, but I don't want them to end up owing their souls to the Notch, or whatever happens if you screw up a bargain. I just want out, and then I can yell at them a lot and all of us can live long enough to fix the mess they've made."

"Does the *succubus* have to be okay—" Candace starts, and there's another knock. It's forceful and decisive, and somehow obviously dramatic in a way that Chloe's knock wasn't, though we might be a little biased. We all look at each other in sudden panic.

Now Chloe hunches. "You can't ignore it. I think it's against the rules."

I can sense the truth of that, and refusing the knock scarcely seems possible. It occurs to me that whatever's on our porch could either break down all my doubts and push me into a new paradigm—or it could be perfectly mundane angry parents threatening to call the cops. I'm not sure which is worse, but not finding out feels like the worst outcome of all. I leave the others in the dining room, and answer the door.

It's not her parents.

The person at the door is tall and lean, wearing a cloak that seems entirely unnecessary even on a day dimming toward thunderstorm. They pull back their hood to reveal anime-sharp cheekbones and piercingly violet eyes, and hair swept back in colors like peacock feathers. Tiny gold chains drape the edges of their elegantly pointed ears. They look like they checked "yes, please" under Gender, and I want to run my fingers along those earlobes, to feel the contrast between smooth warm skin and delicate links of cool metal. I want to taste the lightning on their breath, and the only thing that stops me is the house's anger pouring through from the other direction. I open my mouth, and emit a low growl that's only technically mine.

I will think about all this later.

For now, the—look, all our words are wrong and naming things is dangerous, but not naming things is a pain in the ass so I'm going to call them a succubus for now—the succubus steps back, beautiful eyes widening, and says in a velvet late-night radio voice, "I'm looking for my friend. I'm afraid she might have come here saying some very odd things."

I find my words, barely. "No idea what you're talking about. Go away."

"Please. I'm just trying to help her." They extend their hand (long, graceful fingers beneath the drape of the cloak), and I growl again. I can feel the house so strongly behind me, holding me back from accepting the touch. It feels wolf-like somehow, and irrationally and irrelevantly I recall a joke about werehouses. My brain is juddering in every possible direction. "Can. You. Turn. That. Down?"

"I have no idea what you're talking about." At least they withdraw their hand, fingers sheathed again within the waterfall folds of cloak. Heat lightning illuminates the sky behind them.

"Look," I say. More words now; I'm just going to go with the logic of the situation and worry about everything else later. "We can pretend that I don't know what you are, or what you're trying to do to Ch—" Would saying her name make her vulnerable? That's a thing, right? "—our guest. And you can pretend you don't know what this place is or what kind of protection it offers. Or we can talk like sensible people who both know what's going on, but only if you turn down the weaponized sex appeal, because it does make it very hard to focus."

The succubus frowns, and I catch a flash of their hands again as they rub their wrist nervously. It's a weird bit of body language, less polished and more real. "It's what I am."

Some of the anger is mine, too. "I've had to sit on things that I am for years at a time, just because they made people uncomfortable without interfering even a little bit with their free will. You can manage a few minutes' conversation. Or you can hang out by yourself on the porch and see what the house makes of this whole business. Because right now it kind of wants to go for your throat, and not in a fun way."

The succubus grimaces, rubs their wrist again. They pull the cloak hood over their hair and do *something*, and it does seem to cut the volume. More like watching your favorite celebrity-crush actor playing their perfect role, and less like having them naked in bed with their lips hovering over your own.

"Thank you," I say, because you should always reward people for improving their behavior. "Now. You've been hired to force a relationship with someone who doesn't want it. That's fucked up in so many ways, but the important thing is that you give her parents a refund and leave her alone. I don't know if consent is a thing in fairyland, but around here someone's parents don't get to decide who they kiss, date, or fuck, and neither do you. And she's under our protection." That sounds noble and dramatic, but maybe not sufficiently practical, so I add, "And if you keep stalking her, we're going to find out if the Smith rugby team still moonlights for Whole Man Disposal Services."

"I—" Violet eyes shift nervously under long lashes. Again with the wrist-rubbing; I guess even supernatural incarnations of hotness have nervous tics. "It's more complicated than that. May I please come in and explain?"

This is the unpleasant part, because if Chloe's right—and it's looking increasingly like she understands the nature of the universe a lot better than I do—then I've got to say yes. And hospitality or not, I'm pretty uncomfortable with that.

Candace sidles into the foyer, pausing only a moment as she sees what's on the porch. "Just so you know, we would consider getting someone to do something romantic or sexual with you, even if you can magically make them want it, an insult and a violation of hospitality. Are you sure you want to come in?"

The succubus's throat shivers as they swallow. "That's right, isn't it? Even against my own bargains, the laws of hospitality take priority. Yes. My name is Fiaslet, and I beg the protection of the house."

I swallow, myself. At this point, I can tell, I don't have a choice. Not without losing our ability to shield Chloe. "We offer the house's protection, as you join in providing it. If she doesn't want to be in the same room with you, though, that's her right."

But Chloe stays in the dining room, and meets Fiaslet's eyes and points to the chair farthest from her own, and again I appreciate how she claims her own space. Fiaslet ducks their head and takes the seat as directed. And they keep the volume turned down. I offer the damn succubus banana bread and something to drink; I swear I *am* going to have that existential crisis later, but for now apparently who I am when I believe in magic is someone who feeds people and figures out their evidentiary basis later.

(I am also, it turns out, not entirely over the scientific paradigm, because in addition to the existential crisis and my own insistent libido, the other thing I'm shoving in a box is the running commentary of *this is a non-human intelligence, quick set up a lab and test their working memory capacity.*)

"So," says Del, "what are *you* hiding from?" Which is probably a more urgent question than how human their brain looks. "And also, what are your pronouns? Mine are they/them and I think everyone else here is she/her." Chloe nods confirmation.

Fiaslet smiles distractingly. "Do you know, people don't usually ask me that sort of thing. Whatever pleases you—I like all of them. As for the other thing..." They sigh, and look less pleased. "That's a long story."

"Is it a story that'll help us figure out how to cancel your bargain with my parents?" Chloe demands.

"That's the problem," says Fiaslet. "It's not *my* bargain."

Chloe starts looking less hostile and more interested. She's not the only one. I slide into a chair next to Del and brush their hand for support. "Go on."

Fiaslet stares at us for a minute, and it occurs to me that they probably don't have to explain themself very often.

Finally they start talking, still in that achingly smooth voice that I'd beg to hear narrating a grocery list. But their tone holds an incongruous hint of uncertainty. "I have lived in these mountains for a long time, and for a long time I lived easily. My kind do well alongside humans, and people often sought me when they wished distraction from unwanted passion, or passion from which they could not be distracted, or simply pleasure without the risks of a human mate. And when I needed to hunt, willing partners were still abundant.

"But humans built into the mountains and there were fewer places for us and our cousin kinds, more conflicts over territory and hunting rights. My people are passionate in wars as well as affairs, and I was drawn into a feud. An enemy wounded me gravely, and all the healers had sworn themselves to other powers. So in desperation, I climbed what remains of Round Mountain. You know it?"

It takes me a moment, but Chloe says, "That's where my parents went," and I remember that the mined-out peak atop the Notch has a name.

Fiaslet nods. "Something has dwelled there for a long time, since before I knew this place. But the gravel quarry changed it—corrupted it, or wore it away, or simply gave it power and coldness in trade for its own substance. Now power is all it seeks, and cold bargains are all it offers. It saved my life, and in exchange I became one of the things it could trade." They extend their wrist, and this time I see what they've been rubbing: either a bracelet so tight that it would cut off a human's circulation, or ornately-curlicued gray metal etched like a tattoo into their skin. I whistle softly.

"Does it hurt?" asks Chloe, young and tactless, and Fiaslet tilts their head and says, "That depends on your definition of pain."

After a moment—while I wonder how much Chloe's parents paid—Fiaslet continues: "It seemed fair at the time, part of my life in return for all of it. But the mountain doesn't understand what I am, and doesn't care. It has made my life far less than it was. I am sorry, Chloe." So they do know her name, and I still don't understand the rules under which I'm supposed to protect her. "I would not by my own choice seek prey that did not choose me."

Chloe eyes them cautiously. She takes up her napkin without looking at it, begins folding it into ever-smaller squares. "Why would anyone want to be *prey*?" she asks. "I know what you do. You give pleasure and you steal it. Anything I tried with you, I'd never want with anyone else ever again. Why would someone choose that?"

"Because they wouldn't get a choice," I say, because I'm the only one who saw Fiaslet at full volume. "Hunters have weapons."

Fiaslet closes long lashes, shoulders slumped, and even with the volume down I want to apologize. I resist. "It's not that simple, either," they say.

"I feel," says Candace, "like we've found a whole new axis of unexamined privilege."

Fiaslet's eyes fly open. "You think your species is at some sort of disadvantage here? You think you gained dominion over the mountains and deserts and seas *fairly*?" They catch their breath, shake their head. "When I was free and unencumbered by debt, it was a risk rather than a certainty. Some lovers were never again satisfied with humans, it's true. Others never had been, and hoped I could show them how. Some could hold the memory of a perfect night and still appreciate imperfect ones. You'd go to a restaurant with exquisite cuisine, wouldn't you, and still hunger for lesser tastes?"

"So it's safe to fuck you if we're enlightened enough?" demands Chloe.

"Not now, no. And I have paid the same price: trysts at the mountain's command are pale fare, just enough to keep me alive. It's better, a little, with those who deal for me directly, but your parents are not the first to see me as a tool to direct the passions of others."

I look at our guests, two people in a moment of mutual sympathy and lack of desire, and I want to strangle Chloe's parents. Whether they thought this was some sort of gift or a source of control, whether they panicked or understood exactly what they were doing, I don't understand how she can even think of forgiving them.

She must be feeling something similar, because she pulls from her bag the phone I wasn't sure she had, and powers it on. Which explains how the past couple of hours haven't been a steady stream of frantic notifications. She stabs at her contact list, and of course they pick up on the first ring full of *ohmygodchloewherehaveyoubeenareyouokay*, and she cuts them off with "You knew this was sexual abuse; did you know it was rape the other way too?"

An anxious tenor: "Young lady, it's not any of those things and you know it. You've been so upset and it was obvious that these serial flings aren't good for you, you said so yourself, and we just wanted—"

"You wouldn't surprise me with a puppy because you said it wasn't right to give living things as gifts, but you think I'm going to be thrilled with happy birthday, here's an enslaved sex demon? How much did she cost you?"

"Sweetie, where are you? We—" A higher-pitched voice this time, equally anxious, and Chloe interrupts: "I need to know what you paid, because I need to fix your fuck-up. And then maybe I'll talk to you again before I leave for college."

"Kiddo, this isn't anything you've trained for—"

"Answer the question or get off the phone." They don't, and she does. She glares at the rest of us. "I'm going up the mountain to fix this. Who's helping, and who's trying to talk me out of it?"

"I hate to ask," says Del, "but *are* you trained for this? Whatever 'this' is? Because I'm pretty sure we're not."

"You clearly know the art of claiming yourself," says Fiaslet. "I admire your spirit more than I can say. But the mountain is old, and I've been indebted to it for over a century. You would not be the first to try and get the better of it, but you'd be the first to succeed."

"So your idea is what?" she demands. "We both hide out in the Hearth till I die of old age?"

Candace shrugs. "I'm trained for this. Sort of, anyway. I'm willing to pull out a couple of theses on faerie deals and take the risk."

I raise my hand, tentative and still wondering what the hell I'm doing. "I'm on team make a plan and *then* go up the mountain?"

#

When we head out for the mountain—which was, of course, inevitable—we don't have what I would exactly describe as a plan. We do have some general ideas, a couple of twigs from a decision tree, and approximately the first class session's worth of Bargain Magic 102, as presented by Chloe (age 18, no experience beyond abstract outlines and a lot of warnings) and Fiaslet (age several hundred, considerable experience but most of it with the pointy end). My notes read as follows:

"Narrow path" of how detailed the bargain should be. Need to know what you want, but argue contracts down to the last comma and the genie might screw you over because you left out a comma. The genie will screw you over if you're too vague OR too direct.

Like the house – never insult the entity you're bargaining with, don't do anything they could think of as harm. That gives them permission to mess with you.

You can sell anything, so be careful what you sell.

Everyone involved in a bargain has the right to examine its final form.

And also:

The protection of the hearth holds as long as everyone under it stays together – but weaker than it would be at home. Stay close, and don't say *anything* that could bargain away that protection.

Our plan, such as it is, is to point out that Chloe is involved in this bargain, and has the right to examine all the details. Then we look for alternate interpretations that she and Fiaslet are both okay with—and ideally that give Fiaslet more say in future bargains. It's a pity none of us are lawyers.

I bring along my toolbelt as a sort of symbol of our connection to the house. I don't know whether it will make a difference, but it feels right. Candace puts on her favorite gothic Lolita outfit, black underneath and draped with cobwebs of silver lace. It emphasizes the space she takes up, and how good she looks taking it. Del sticks with their hypothetical ghost outfit on the theory that changing would be an even worse omen than keeping it on. We all crowd into Candace's station wagon, giving Fiaslet shotgun because no one wants to ruin themselves for all future instances of being crowded together in the back seat.

The thunderheads have darkened by the time we leave, rain starting to splatter the walk and lightning throwing droplets into relief against the windshield. This happens more summer afternoons than not: from the right vantage, you can watch storms glide over the mountains, trailing kaleidoscopes of light and shadow across their contours. From there you can see how the rain cuts off with sketch-sharp edges, how any vulnerability to the pathetic fallacy depends on an extremely narrow point of view. The weather shouldn't be ominous. But I'm already thinking about how mud washes across Route 116 like ice where it rises over the Notch.

I spent so long in Boston, surrounded by the grappling architectural tentacles of rival universities. It's still strange, sometimes, how the Valley's colleges settle into oases amid the gentler anthropocene scatter, how there remains so much room for mountain and forest in between. Probably it it's different for Chloe, who's never lived elsewhere, or for

Fiaslet, who knew the place and its people before Geoffrey Amherst claimed and broke the land with deadly gifts. But Amherst's namesake campus squats amid old Victorians and cute restaurants, only a brief umbra of town beyond its edges before you hit trees again. That neat, civilized surface should strain and stretch with the pressures beneath. Why isn't *this* place haunted?

Past Amherst, the road winds through verdant pine and oak and maple, rushing streams and little mills. Fiaslet leans against the window, cloak hiding their unearthly beauty. Squashed between me and Dell, shoulders pulled in tight, Chloe has taken a square of origami paper from her backpack and begun folding something complicated. I mull over what I've seen, seeking discontinuities from what I've been told. I'm supposed to be the scientist, the skeptic. But I'm having trouble untangling feeling and observation from interpretation. Maybe my sense of the house as a living entity is just my own overenthusiastic mental modeling. Maybe Fiaslet hails from some odd corner of humanity, evolved to absurd levels of facial symmetry and, I don't know, blah blah pheromones. I haven't seen anything that violates conservation of mass.

Then again, there's no reason that something has to actively break the laws of physics to count as magic. Magic could do all sorts of impossible-seeming things, and still end up on the back road to quantum mechanics. I'm in no position to tell what's really unbelievable on that level; the part that most breaks *my* science is the idea that a house, or a mountain, could have self-awareness and cognitive processes.

All of which I'm hamstering over because I feel like I should. Not because it makes it any easier to deal with the problem. We slip by the next oasis—Hampshire's 60s-era dorms and sheep pastures—and then the trees close in, the timpani raindrops turn into a downpour, and something old, interested, and malicious is paying attention. Candace grips the steering wheel. Even at 15 miles an hour, the car shudders against the road. We cling to the ground, trying to ignore the warning rattle of the rain.

The mountain levels off abruptly, and the trees break for a blacktop lot that I've never actually pulled into before. It never seemed like a good idea, and it doesn't now. But here we are, and rain tapers into mizzle—not exactly a welcome, but permission, even invitation, to leave the safety of the car. Fiaslet opens their door with the banal resignation of someone going to meet a particularly rigid department chair. Chloe squeezes out behind them, leaving a crisp paper frog in the back seat, and the rest of us follow. My glasses fog instantly, and I take them off to let them clear. In my blurred vision, eyelashes already matting, the old warehouses and piles and pits seem broken from ordinary scale, improbably large or absurdly tiny.

When we were in college the lot was gravel. Abandoned equipment rusted at its edge, towering in the corners of vision every time I drove by. Sometime while we were in thrall to our dream jobs, the quarry company returned to dismantle their industrial ruins, shove the worst of the mess into the warehouses, and mark the entrance with a clean marble sign. It probably improved the safety of local wildlife and maybe Umass fratboys as well. But now, as I blink water from my eyes, the clean lot feels like a mask. I blink again and ragged white metal rises through the mist: lines broken by the chains of an old lift, by dangling ropes and wires, by the serpentine curve of the gravel chute. I move toward the impossible structure, hoping the others are with me but unable to look away. I can feel its claws deep in the earth, the power that leveled a mountain. The power that *allowed* the mountain to be leveled. That wanted the deal more than it wanted to *be* a mountain.

"You see that?" asks Del, and I nod without shifting my gaze.

"Me too," says Candace. Her voice is even steadier than usual, covering for fear. Shared delusions are common as dirt; shared hallucinations are mostly not a thing that happens.

We're close now, in the ghostly shadow of a ghostly structure. I try to speak and cough instead, lick my lips, try again. "Hello. Thank you for taking the time to see us. I'm Leah, the... a keeper of the Hearth, and we've given our protection to Chloe and Fiaslet. We'd like to talk."

Somehow the mist both muffles my words and echoes them, so they return sounding no longer quite mine. From the drifts of white and gray, a shape accumulates. A man—or something very like one—steps forward. His skin is pale gray and his suit is dark gray, and he wears a hungry gray smile below cold gray eyes and the pencil slash of his nose. He offers me his fog-fleshed hand; his smile broadens as I take it reluctantly. That reluctance, I hope, won't count as insult on its own. His grip is cold but solid.

"It's been a long time since the Hearth graced us with a visit. You are *most* welcome." His voice is—not gray, in fact, but deep and confident, just rough enough to be interesting. "But why on earth would these two require your protection? Chloe's parents came to me seeking a way to ease her pain, and I provided even more than they originally asked. I offered the services of a treasured member of our family— one of my dearest vassals." He lifts an arm, and Fiaslet slips deferentially into his grip. Only their eyes lack surrender. "Surely my beloved servant, and a girl fortunate enough to be granted his attentions, have no need for guards?"

Candace shoots me a frightened, urgent look, and I swallow back my first response. Prodded, I spot the trap. The truth about why we've offered sanctuary would, as he's framed it, insult him and his wares. And any agreement with his claims, if not phrased extremely carefully, might retract that sanctuary.

"It sounds like you've been generous," Candace says. "And you've told us your relationship to Chloe and Fiaslet—so we've explained ours."

"Only," says Chloe, less smoothly, and certainly not sounding *not scared*, "I'd like to understand what my parents bought for me."

The gray man raises a gray eyebrow. "The specifics of a bargain are usually between seller and customer."

"The details of a bargain should be clear to everyone involved. It was a gift for me, so I'm involved. So's Fiaslet, for that matter." She smiles at the succubus, hopefully in a way that suggests to the gray man that they're doing their job. "If you promised their, um, attentions, they're very much involved in the agreement."

"Hmmm. I suppose that makes sense." He releases Fiaslet, crouches, and begins drawing curling labyrinths in the mist. The shapes remind me, uncomfortably, of Fiaslet's tattoo. "And what of the Hearth—do you claim some involvement in this bargain as well? Apparently it encompasses more than I knew."

I glance at Candace, but she doesn't seem to have intuited the right answer. I hedge. "Only the connection we described earlier."

He hums again, but seems to decide that we get to watch. The lines expand, grow three-dimensional and complex as a mad scientist's equation. I can almost read meaning, connections suggesting flows of demand and energy. Del circles with a sculptor's avid gaze.

"Here is the detail you're due," the gray man tells Chloe. He stands too close, not-breathing into her ear as he leans over her shoulder. Mist clings dankly against my neck. "Do you know the language of the contract?"

She shakes her head—no way to deny ignorance, with this thing hanging in front of us.

The gray man smiles possessively at Fiaslet. "Explain it, then. That seems within the remit of your obligations."

Before any of us can object, he takes Fiaslet's hand and Chloe's, pressing them together. They spring apart, Chloe turning to glare at him, and he smirks coldly. "Fiaslet..." I flinch at the warning in his voice, and Chloe's eyes widen.

I know I can't object directly to his "generosity." But I've got to say something, or our protection becomes meaning-less. "Surely there's no insult in making use of a gift at one's own pace," I try. "Or in Fiaslet respecting how she uses what she's been given."

The gray man frowns, but gestures brusquely at the succubus without arguing further. Fiaslet traces the diagram with an elegant finger. Their arm passes through the mist as they prod its inner workings, disrupting nothing. "This describes us and our connections: my relationship to the mountain, yours to your parents. And ours to each other, created by the contract: the agreement is that we are to *have* a relationship. That I will give you pleasure and companion-ship, and shield you from loneliness and heartbreak due to the actions of others—and this, here, shows how my obliga-tion to do so descends from my obligation to the mountain. And how—ah—your obligation to accept descends from your obligation to your parents."

"Wait a second," Chloe shields her hand where Fiaslet touched it. "They can promise to make me do something? What the everloving fuck?"

"One's firstborn is a customary cost: the child in all its parts, flesh and thought and spirit." The gray man speaks as if lecturing on a fine point of theory, but his lips quirk. "This is much more moderate, requiring only a portion of flesh and thought."

"I'm 18 next month! They can't just give me away!"

"You are still their firstborn, still theirs to direct under the law of the contract."

Fiaslet steps in before Chloe can escalate with who-knows-what consequence. "And here is the seal, a promise between your parents and the mountain that they will both fulfill their ends of the bargain. That if the mountain fails to provide—me, and my services—a portion of its power will be forfeit to your parents, in the form of a favor and a gift. And that if your parents fail to provide you—your flesh and mind as described in the contract—then they will likewise owe compensation. Which would, of course, make up a greater portion of their power than the mountain's." They pause, and their voice takes on an ironic lilt. "Traditionally, if one fails to fulfill a contract due to the failure of one's vassals, the cost of compensation is passed first *to* those vassals. Drawn from their power and life force, however much or little they have to give."

The gray man turns his insincere smile on Fiaslet. "Your work on this contract has been unusually slow, I must say. Perhaps you might speed it up to ensure that such a failure *doesn't* come to pass."

They don't move. "There's no timetable. And she *wants* to go slowly."

"There is no grace on the terms, either. If you allow her to suffer loneliness or heartbreak, you have failed."

Fiaslet's drawn-in shoulders, the rigidness of their stance beneath the cloak, suggest that they expect *some* sort of failure. Their glamour, which they've been holding in check all this time, spills across the lot. They're beautiful again, desperately and painfully, drawing everyone toward them save the gray man himself. This time, though, I recognize it as defensive reflex, like a skunk's odor, instinctive and mis-placed. They close their eyes. "Give me time, I beg of you, to do this right."

The gray man's voice goes quiet, a knife-blade's distance above a whisper. "I have given you life. I determine how our contractual obligations are to be met. I direct you in ways that go far beyond this one contract, and you will *not* skimp on your debt."

The mist seems to crystallize, interlocking symbols stretching around us in a cage of contracts, obligations, structures of debt and demand looming above and closing us in. Fiaslet flinches. Then their eyes grow unfocused, and they begin pacing toward Chloe. She backs up, but slowly, caught in the fascination of the succubus's presence. And I sense, too, that retreat would risk losing ourselves in the gray man's bargain-built web.

I can only think of one way to protect Chloe, and it's stupid. But giving up on that protection would leave all five of us desperately vulnerable, and anyway it's so easy, so tempting, that I'm already moving to block Fiaslet's path, to hurl myself into their startled embrace. I'm drowning, overwhelmed by their scent even before they press their lips against mine. I run my fingers along their earlobe and feel the cool loops of chain against silken skin.

But it's *me* they're kissing, not Chloe, not one of the gray man's unwilling targets. They whimper into our shared breath and I wonder, faintly, how long it's been since they've kissed without the gray man's order and approval.

And then—I'm no longer drowning. I'm no longer alone in Fiaslet's embrace. Something warm and strong fills the contours of my mind, all hardwood and metal and flickering hearthfire. I let the house brace my will and the kiss softens to glorious, bearable embers. Fiaslet pulls back, eyes their own again and glowing with pleasure.

The gray man's voice comes like a lash. "How dare the Hearth interfere in my business?" I feel—something, the power in his words perhaps—slice against the walls shielding my mind. Fiaslet gasps and shudders.

"They're under our protection," I say. But we've insulted him now, haven't we? Violated *his* hospitality, such as it was, and I don't know what that lets him do to us. I don't know what he can do to Fiaslet and Chloe, tangled as they are in the choking equations of his contract. Fiaslet is shaking. The house stretches its power to cover us, but we're miles from home, at the heart of our enemy's power, and the strain swells against my skull, pressure on the verge of becoming pain.

The gray man looks at Chloe. "You are new to being a vassal, and I would treasure a loyal sorcerer, but I expect my people to learn quickly. And you—" to Fiaslet. "—this is not the first time you've underperformed. I expect better, and I will have it. You both have 24 hours to do as the contract requires, before I collect on the forfeit you owe me for its failure."

"But *you* won't have failed it!" Chloe accuses.

"Nor do I intend to. That is why I give my people additional deadlines beyond what I owe others." His mist-gray lips quirk again, an expression I'm coming to dread. "It's simply good management."

This feels like a good time to pretend cooperation and get out of here, but Chloe's far beyond her earlier caution, trembling with fear and fury. "I won't! I didn't agree to this, I don't belong to my parents, and I don't belong to you either! This is a mistake and I want out!"

The haze of symbols snaps fully into focus around us, cage sharpening to razor-wire bars. The gray man stalks toward Chloe and I grab her without thinking. "Come on!" I call to the others, still afraid to move but even more afraid not to. The house is still trying to help, and we need to stay close together, be a hearth even here, far from the literal walls keeping our wills intact. Del and Candace are beside us, joining the line of hands with that too-weak power flowing between them. I grab Fiaslet and feel again the jolt of desire. The sensuality's incongruous now, but its own barrier against the calculations crowding around us. My fingers brush their bound wrist and it burns like ice. We race for the car.

Retreat's as terrifying as I expected: the gray man's contracts throng the air, symbols that blur my vision and mire my legs, making me run nightmare-slow. I should be able to tell pain from terror, but I can't. Maybe something's actually cutting the backs of my hands and stifling my breath, or maybe it's only my mind filled with choking shame. I've failed an obligation forced on me by someone else, someone whose opinion I care about desperately. We have professors who've never taken a sick day in twenty years, who take their teaching obligations seriously, who would never miss a grading deadline or neglect a request from a friend or get to the hospital too late, too late—but I still have Chloe's hand and Fiaslet's, can still feel warmth from the embers in the fireplace, and I think I'm still running. We stagger at last against the car. Someone gets the doors open and I tumble into the back seat, Fiaslet on one side slumping against the window with harsh breaths while Chloe sobs on my other.

"Oh god, I'm sorry, I can't—" Del gasps in the shotgun seat while Candace fumbles the key. Candace is humming, high and desperate and panicked, and I lean forward to grab her shoulder and urge as much of the house's protection as we can spare to her reflexes.

As she squeals us out of the lot, too fast, the rain's already sheeting down, no pathetic fallacy but the gray man's anger. Trees crowd close, and wheels slip on the muddy road. The car slides sideways, veers back, splashes through a pothole puddle and sprays the windshield to whiteout. The wipers whip back sight, fighting for glimpses of the road.

"Slow," says Del urgently. "We've got to go slow, if we get in an accident—"

"I *know*!" Candace grips the wheel. "I'm *trying*! Fiaslet, turn it the fuck down."

"*I'm* trying." They bow head over knees, clutching their wrist where the contract chains it. I rub their back with my free hand, because at this point why the hell not? The pressure of their presence eases a fraction. They're still shaking.

The wheels grind against the road now through the mud, but going slow is as hard psychologically as it must be for Candace physically. The usual sense of malice along this stretch has gone from whisper to scream. Every moment that we're here I can feel—not hatred, something colder and less personal—I can feel the gray man's desire to own us prodding our defenses, despising them and determined to crack them open.

We're almost past the Notch's shadow when rain slams into us like a wall. I can't see anything through the windshield but water, and my hand tightens on Candace's shoulder. The wheels skid and she steers against it—and I'm caught hyper-aware in the moment when they fail to find purchase. The car spins across the road in slow motion, riding a slick of mud through the too-slight resistance of floodwater, and my first second's prayer—"please get us out of here alive, please get us out"—transmutes to repeating, to myself or to the universe, "I am the keeper of the hearth, I am the keeper of the hearth." That mantra grows. I'm saying it out loud, shouting it—"I am the keeper of the hearth!"—and I feel the house straining to reach us, to understand the danger of movement far outside its experience, and I grab onto the stillness and the solidity of its foundation and pull as hard as I can—

And the car slides to a stop at the foot of the slope. It takes me a moment to believe we're still alive, still upright, haven't hit anything. Candace and Chloe are crying and Del stares, shockily, in a way I don't like. Fiaslet is folded up on themself, head curled into their knees, and it takes another moment to recognize incongruous horniness through the haze of other reasons for my heart to race.

I shake their shoulder. "Fiaslet, we're okay. Goddammit, do you have *any* way to handle danger without trying to seduce it?"

They turn their head to glare up through long lashes. "I don't know, monkey, do you have any way to handle danger without yelling and throwing shit?"

"I did not *throw shit*—" I take a deep breath, trying to hold down the monkey instinct, and feel the projection recede again. Both projections—the rain still hammers the roof, but at a more comprehensible rate, and that sense of all-encompassing fury has receded. Out of range, or else the gray man's made his point, coiled back up in his mineshaft to wait for us to mend our ways.

Chloe sniffs, peers around me, and asks Fiaslet, "Aren't you a primate too? You look pretty hominid-ish."

They sit up slowly, grimacing at some lingering pain. "Next time I seduce an evolutionary biologist, I'll ask them to research my ancestry. Are we—?" They glance behind us, as if unsure how to finish the sentence.

I lean forward to hug Candace. "Are you okay? Are you hurt?"

She shakes her head. "Just terrified. I don't think we hit anything; I don't know if the tires are okay; I don't want to get out and check."

It's easier to be the problem-solver, to break the impossible down into practical decisions. "If the tires go round and round, they'll probably get us home. We can check everything else once we're there. Do you need someone else to drive?"

Candace looks at the three of us crowded into the back seat, and at Del. She reaches tentatively for their hand, rubs it, and Del blinks and shakes their head.

"Sorry," they say, "that was, um, I can drive if you need me to? If we can switch around without getting out?"

Candace is five feet even and has the seat crammed forward to reach the pedals, the steering wheel dropped as low as it will go without crowding her tits. Del's almost a foot taller and usually spends five solid minutes after a switch-off readjusting the seat and swearing. And no one wants to take over *my* spot. I can see them both making the mental calculations.

"I'll do it," Candace decides. "Give me a second." She puts on the hazard lights, then pulls out her phone and opens the meditation app. "You all—talk about *something*."

I should probably find a painless distraction, but what pops out of my mouth is, to Fiaslet: "What did he do to you back there?"

They look down at their hands. "Not much, really. Just reminded me what I owe." They see my failure to parse that, and go on: "My injuries are not truly healed. Only in abeyance. He can return them to me at will, temporarily, to remind me that he could do so permanently if he wished." After a moment (which I don't find any way to fill), they add, "I believe he makes use of my injuries to discipline others, as well. When he perceives the need."

Chloe shudders, not quite shrinking back but keeping my body as a shield between them. "That's what he's going to do if—if you don't seduce me?"

"He would probably not allow me to die," says Fiaslet. Their voice is very even. "He wouldn't wish to lose a valuable resource. But he is, as he says, growing tired of how I resist my obligations. I'm of little value if that resistance continues."

"Little value to *him*," I put in, reflexively, and they flash a joyless smile.

"It isn't right!" says Chloe with childish righteousness. "He's awful!" She clenches her fists in her lap. Then, not childishly at all, she goes on, "I need to do this. It's not like I've got a girlfriend I'd be giving up. It's not right, to let you get hurt because I'm waiting for something I might not even find."

"No!" Fiaslet's refusal overlaps with my own. We look at each other and Fiaslet goes on, "Maybe I should. Give in. Wait for a chance to push back when I won't be hurting anyone else. Because he will, he'll punish you too. Put the cost of his default on me, and of your parents' on you."

"No," I repeat. Somewhere on the mountain, arguing with the monster I wasn't supposed to believe in, I traded away my doubt for fear. The gray man terrifies me, but if he's there then I know what I have to be. "You two are not sacrificing yourselves to each other to keep some god-damned—" What is he? Chloe warned us about terms—crossroads devil? Fair folk? "—supernatural payday lender comfortable. We're going back to the house, and we're finding another way."

#

We get home—rain at a perfectly reasonable drizzle, car doing car things, but Candace shivers the whole way and I just feel hideously vulnerable. I've been trying to hold everyone together, but I want to crawl into a box and hide somewhere dark and safe.

We stumble onto the porch and I fumble with the lock, get us inside at last. I can barely see for the house's sudden, overwhelming relief: a friend's hug after you come home from the hospital, a dog leaping up to greet you when you've been gone all day, an anxious mother checking for scrapes after a nasty fall on the playground. I plop down in the middle of the foyer, accepting its attentions. I let it examine the razor cuts to mind and body, flinching despite myself when the pain goes deeper, while I run my fingers over the varnished floor.

"What precisely the hell happened here?" asks Candace. At that point I finally raise my head and start paying attention with my normal senses: the house looks like the storm hit it *inside*. Food and papers and tools and even a couple of chairs have fallen across the floor, and at least one precarious pile of boxes has collapsed. Amid the mess, flame flickers in the fireplace. I stacked a log and some kindling in there a few days ago, fantasizing about winter comfort—but didn't go as far as, say, buying matches. Nevertheless it burns.

A bit primly, but mostly with the false evenness of shock, I offer: "I had to grab on really tightly during the accident?"

We all stare at the fire, and after a few minutes Candace starts picking up papers and righting furniture, and Dell goes into the kitchen and comes back with a carving fork to serve as a poker and make sure the magically-lit fire is sturdily stacked—though I'd hope a house stressed enough to light its own hearth is cautious enough to keep itself safe.

Fiaslet hangs their sodden cloak by the door, and they and Chloe help with the cleaning. Her body language is abrupt, mechanical, while theirs is smooth in a way I'm coming to recognize as equally tense. Eventually we all end up back at the table, chairs angled toward the fireplace like iron filings magnetized by the glow. Del adds another log as the first burns down. The rainwashed breeze wafts through the window and it's still too hot, but the fire feels necessary.

Sarcasm crowds my tongue—'That could have gone better' and 'Your boss is almost as bad as my old department chair'—but our failure looms too heavily. Tomorrow afternoon, precise moment unknown because I failed to check the time while dealing with the devil, something terrible will happen to Chloe and Fiaslet. Unless they do something terrible to each other first.

"I don't know what tools we have to handle this," I admit. "We may be keepers of the hearth, but we're not trained, and I have no idea how far the house's protection stretches. If you stay here tomorrow, will we be able to keep you safe?"

Fiaslet, arms tightly wound, leans in toward the heat and the magic. Their hair dries in tangled waves. I see now how they're always hiding their wrist, always worrying it. "I don't know. Not easily. The mountain will fight to fulfill its word. It is far older than the Hearth, and though it's strongest in its own place, the contracts spread its power. It doesn't taper as quickly as yours. It may send agents first, but if those fail it must enforce its claims personally, or lose them. And the Hearth must fulfill *your* identity, or be broken. I'm sorry; I've brought great trouble on you."

"Technically that was me," Chloe puts in.

I'm far more frightened than I was this time yesterday, and in more real danger. Without our visitors I'd be finishing up the doorknobs about now: reasonably content, unsure of what I was building beyond those moment-to-moment repairs. Part of me is awake that I didn't know existed. I feel lit to burning by this more urgent repair—whether or not it's possible, whether or not the crack is too wide to mend. "You told us that the Hearth has an identity to lose. That's worth a great deal."

Restless, I rise to pace the room, looking for work. I settle on the windows, where the paint around the frame still needs touching up. It may be meaningless in the grand scheme of tomorrow's confrontation, but it's a way of returning the house's care. The plasticky hot-car scent of paint mixes with burning wood, and I imagine the smoke sinking in as the paint dries, a bit of the house's own magic spackled back into its chinks. What will the Mountain's agents do, when they come? Will they cast curses, or just bring guns and matches? If they're bent on ordinary mortal harm, there's not much we can do to stop them.

I dip the brush, wipe excess paint against the can lip. "How *can* we protect ourselves?"

"We tried beating the mountain under its own rules," says Del. "It didn't work."

"It felt like filling out paperwork for an adjunct position." Candace's voice is muffled, and when I check over my shoulder she's kneeling on her chair, chin tucked into her arms on the table. She looks shaken still. Her lace skirt dries stiffly against her ankles.

"Yeah." Del nods, fidgets. "For all this has been the second-most-impossible day of my life, I feel like I've just spent three hours filling out badly-designed insurance forms while stuck in a phone tree."

I finish the one side of the frame, and shift position. I prod my own emotions. "It feels like both, to me. Learning about the Hearth's purpose is... big, like quitting my job. But

44

trying to talk the gray man around, that felt like all the things that make the world small."

"It's what it does," says Fiaslet. "It makes things smaller and duller, even itself, to become more powerful." I can't imagine why it would choose to be an asshole, when it could have been one of the Berkshires' autumn-gilded peaks. Not that I'm any expert on cognitive geology.

Fiaslet goes on, "At its best, the magic of exchange is rich with meaning and glory. It can be two entities sharing what's best of themselves, weaving a bond of debt and duty and passion, passing vulnerability between them like wine. I should have died, rather than bind myself to something so inimical to my nature."

I want to put down the paintbrush and give them a hug. But I don't know whether it would be welcome, what the others would think of my touching Fiaslet for simple comfort rather than in the midst of magical confrontation, or even whether the house would be irritated by my taking its protection for granted. "I'm glad you're alive."

They shrug, lips quirking. "Many people feel otherwise."

"I'm glad too," says Chloe, "even if I still don't want to fixate on you like a creepily sexualized duckling."

"There's an image," says Fiaslet. "Quack." They both snicker. She pinches her hands into a beak and giggles—looking even more painfully young than she is.

The house could protect her from Fiaslet's glamour, of course, as it does me. But even if they wanted to handle things that way, it wouldn't meet either of their obligations—even more than the sex, it's the dependency that her parents dealt for, a parodic shadow of what a relationship would look like with both parties willing.

I feel my way around a landscape I still don't understand. "There's nothing, is there, like the way that married people don't have to testify against each other in court? No sort of deal that can overrule the ones already in place?"

"Not that I know of," says Chloe, and Fiaslet shakes their head.

"What about the other kind of magic? Our kind, that made the Hearth?"

"It's different," says Chloe, "but I don't know what it can do against deals. I've never heard of anyone trying, but my parents haven't exactly given me the whole manual."

She looks at Fiaslet. They chew on their lip as they consider, a weirdly endearing moment of gracelessness. "Claiming oneself, defining identity, is a human art. Others can practice it, but the masters are almost exclusively among your kind. I was always told that this is because the first masters of the art were human, and were able to define selfhood as a human thing—to ensure that no human can redefine another."

It only takes a moment. "But we can redefine non-humans," I say, feeling queasy.

"It's harder than with a house or an animal," they say. "We can defend ourselves. But we're vulnerable, and humans have certainly taken advantage."

Candace lifts her head. "Could we redefine the mountain? Sorry, that's probably very evil, and I promise I would feel bad afterward."

"It could defend itself *very* well," Fiaslet points out. "Especially given the number of human workers who owe it debts, Chloe's parents not least. And I'm confident that none of *you* are masters at the art."

Candace subsides. "Here I already had plans for my supervillain outfit."

"So what *can* we do?" I ask again.

My notes for Identity Magic 102—as presented by Chloe (age 18, homeschooled on the topic by a couple of clearly-unreliable experts) and Fiaslet (age several hundred, knows a few things but has mostly been warned about the pointy end)— read as follows:

Less rule-bound and more intuitive—you define the symbols of identity at the same time as you define the identity.

Can't define other humans. Non-humans, who actually do have personal identities despite the magic not recognizing them—what the fuck, creepy ancient master mages—are likely to fight back, possibly by stabbing you before you can redefine them as someone who wouldn't stab you.

Claiming your own selfhood can be even more dangerous, because if you try to make too big a change, if you try to claim an identity that actively contradicts your innermost truths, *you'll* fight back.

It's not, as it turns out, something that actually lends itself well to bullet points. But some remnant of academia is still part of *my* selfhood, and that part takes notes when trying to solve problems.

"Maybe we can shore up our identities somehow, or the house's?" I ask. The bullet points spread into doodles in my notebook, galactic spirals rippling out along the page and dripping into vines, into fractal leaves shaped like tiny flames. "Act like ourselves really hard, and give ourselves more to work with tomorrow?"

It feels cheesy, but Chloe is nodding along. "My parents do something like that. If they have a big working coming up, they put on a party where everyone dresses up and shows off." She blushes suddenly. "No offense, but please tell me you're all into tamer parties than my folks? I mean, drugs are a good way to lower your inhibitions and act more like yourself, I guess, but I usually go upstairs at that point and play my favorite music really loudly. There are people I just don't want to see making out."

"Sounds awfully Crowley-ish," says Candace.

"I mean yes, that's where the tradition comes from, and also fuck the British Empire," says Chloe. I guess magic "workers" are up there with Neopagans for having strong views on 19th Century cult leaders. Not that I'm personally short on opinions about either Crowley's fashion sense or his basic grasp of consent, mostly based on Candace's rants.

"We're not big drinkers," says Del, "and I definitely don't want to magically reinforce my stoned level of stupidity. But music works, and I could paint something?"

"In here!" I wave my hands at the blank wall where we've talked about hanging a tapestry. "We could make a mural—Candace's storytelling, your art, my, um, I realize home improvement is not the most excitingly Bohemian demonstration of identity, but I'm not actually an excitingly Bohemian girl."

Chloe thinks this sounds like the kind of party she can get behind—and Fiaslet may be a club-hunting sex elemental who'd be happier at an orgy, but they approve the plan as well. After all, we're strengthening ourselves to shore up the house that's striving to protect us. A house-decorating party seems appropriate.

#

We break off to find the things we need. The things we feel like we need. Intuitive, right? I can do intuitive.

I can't do intuitive. Or at least, I never have. I planned my career carefully from the moment I took my first Intro Psych class—fall in love with one lecture on conversational pragmatics, pay for a lifetime. I set priorities, laid out schedules for running studies and writing articles, met my self-imposed deadlines. Considered for every relationship whether it fit that vision, and whether the precise strength of my feelings justified changing plans. I don't want to sound like a "career woman" from some made-for-tv Christmas movie, discovering at the feet of a rugged country man that love is more important. It's that I never asked myself if my life felt whole and right, instead of just like the logical endpoint of all my classes. For some people the logical endpoint is also the fulfilling one. But I didn't go deep enough to do that.

It turns out that, for me, *fulfilling* has to use my whole body, make it obvious that my mind isn't some separate abstraction. I want roses that scrape my palms and cast their scent across the yard, hardwood grain broadcasting its texture through coats of varnish. I want emotions big enough to make me desperate to act instead of desperate for excuses not to. But I've barely started practicing that kind of life— now I have to do it well enough to make the universe act on my desires too.

I dig through boxes of clothing before deciding that the dirt of the day *is* what I want to wear. Del and Candace are both fashion mavens whose carefully-designed outfits show off their innermost selves. You can be just as deliberate dressing like a butch handywoman, but what I want more than any specific shirt is the smudged knees from where I knelt to fix the doorknob, the mud of the mountain, grit still in my hair and cuts stinging my elbows, the place where paint spattered my t-shirt. I want work that marks me.

I do strap my toolbelt back on, stopping first to breathe in the well-worn leather. Hammer, screwdriver, pockets for different sizes of nails and screws so you can find the right one to meet each moment's need. Little solutions, sharp and solid.

Back downstairs, I clear boxes away from our blank wall. We've already painted it a cheerful yellow, and there's no time to lay down a coat of white for a fresh canvas, but maybe this is better: building on what's gone before. I spread out cloth, find brushes that are probably entirely wrong for whatever Del will want to do. In the living room, Chloe is head-tilt scanning the bookshelves that we *have* unpacked, humming quietly to herself.

Candace comes down in her second-favorite Lolita dress, this one all-over vintage prints of whales and tentacles and compasses. It's got some sort of boning, too, pushing up her

J-cup breasts with architectural discipline. She's pinned her hair in an elaborately beaded net, and she's got one of her more portable drums tucked under her arm. (Her last school let her hold a late-night bonfire for her 400-level class, drumming and singing so they'd feel how the stories are supposed to sound. Once, and then the university lawyers caught up with the idea.) She settles herself carefully at the table and taps a quick rhythm, testing. "At least now if I have to go begging to my parents, they won't be able to follow my life choices well enough to tell me how stupid they were."

"Your parents can keep their opinions to themselves," I suggest automatically. They're perfectly decent people. They love Candace. They just don't understand—well. They aren't our problem tonight, and if we can make this whole thing work, maybe not ever.

"I'll ignore their opinions when this country gets a real safety net," she returns automatically, distracted by the drum. She starts singing, no words yet, just nonsense syllables weaving around Chloe's hum and the tap-ta-ta-dum-ta, tap-ta-ta-dum-ta, and I sway to whatever's building.

Then I catch my breath as Del and Fiaslet come downstairs. Del looks splendid as always, dress traded out for tight jeans and a magenta sleeveless shirt-tunic thing that shows off the rainbow of wheat and corn decorating their upper arms. They've got amazing biceps suitable for painting a much larger wall, or for the metalwork sculpture that's their other favored form.

But Fiaslet. They've obviously been at Del's closet, and the clothes that help a human mark territory outside the binary also show off a body that's never been near it. A black dress drops into a knee-length rag skirt flaring in shades of ocean. It complements their peacock hair and shows off long legs shimmering with the same iridescence. Their bare feet are tipped with rounded claws rather than nails. The house is protecting me and I still want them, no magic to it beyond the magnetism of someone being beautifully and unapologetically themself. They sway to Candace's beat, and their fingers trace little spirals in the air without straying to their wrist.

Chloe spins over. She closes her eyes, making space for herself in the corner of the room. Her expression is fierce, concentrated, the way you look when you're getting something you need in the midst of pain. I try to let go too, to dance without analyzing everyone else's dancing, but it's hard. Chloe's movements are self-contained, without any apparent care for witnesses. Fiaslet dances for everyone, with us or at us, the opposite of self-contained and yet just as certain. If I breathe myself a moment between thoughts, I can let them take up the space in my head that's trying to cushion everything with words. I can dance with them, and then with Del who they're also dancing with, with the table and the hearth and the walls that shape the space we move through: the warm shelter and food and art that are the practical seeds of this magic. There's a pattern growing here, in ourselves and our space and our movement. I'm reaching for something exactly unlike the gray man's contracts, lines that connect without constraining, that map possibilities rather than boundaries, if only I could bring them into focus...

Candace's wordless tune grows words: true to her practice, she's found ballads to fit the story we're trying to tell. She starts with "Tam Lin," one of the bouncier versions, lingering on the Hallow's Eve rescue and holding the young knight through transformations to lion and snake and fire. I recognize the next song from the semester when she was memorizing all the Child Ballads, a woman freeing herself by answering the devil's riddles. Other clever mortals follow: winning fiddle contests with fairie queens, tricking gods into sharing power, retrieving things irretrievably lost. I know, from Candace's complaints that semester, that these are rare gems surrounded by songs of brother killing sister, deadly pregnancies, hateful families. But that's the magic, right? The power that Chloe told us about, to make room for the stories we choose instead of bending to stories forced on us by others.

The image comes to me as it comes to Del, maybe to all of us at once. Del's the one to pick up brush and paint, but it's sharp in my mind as our dance fleshes it out, as they begin sketching.

I don't know how long we dance. It's been years since I've truly gotten away from time, from schedules and looming deadlines. Our failure to check clocks on the mountain doesn't count—that place was all deadline. Even during the pandemic, when everyone I knew outside of academia complained of calendars grown meaningless, I was constantly aware of every class and grading due date and the ticking tenure clock. I lost *space*, the whole planet compressed to my studio apartment and computer screen, forgetting what countries my students peered through from, but time kept its dominance. Now, though, I'm dancing and drawing and drumming and singing and feeling the heat of fire and bodies. And even though I share those senses with four others, I'm also feeling exquisitely myself: someone who fixes problems and welcomes the people who come with those problems, and someone who is alive in a room with my oldest and newest friends.

Legs aching, I find time again slowly and comfortably, leaning against the wall beside the hearth and looking over the table at our mural. Del's draped across a chair, creation done, and Chloe lies nearby. Candace taps out a quiet rhythm, easing us down. Only Fiaslet stands, still swaying, and I sense through the remains of our dance a fear of what will return when they stop. But they're looking too.

What we've made is shaped by Del's hand and Del's style: an impressionist splash of colors with corners of strange realism. A person—features obscured by brush-spatters of flowing hair—embraces flame. That much must be inspired by Tam Lin, but I don't see Janet enduring the blistering pain of her lover's curse. This flame holds its heat at a blue core, and the human figure reaches out eagerly, power mirrored in their own palette of indigo and gold. There are hints, too, of other figures—maybe the fire has more than one companion, more than one willing embrace. The real fire nibbles its last log, and the imagined one proclaims the real one's purpose. Our purpose.

Chloe blinks up through narrow eyes, grinning. "Not bad for a first try."

It's grown dark outside, and I can feel tomorrow lying in wait. Candace brings the drumming to a close at last. I'm watching Fiaslet, and see how they slump as the ritual falls away, how they force themself back upright to hide it.

"Whatever happens next, we're going to need sleep, yeah?" Candace asks.

"Hold up." Del wipes their hands and goes into the kitchen. I hear water running, and the fridge door, and they come out with a loaf of bread—store-bought challah from a couple days ago, but still good. We pass it around, not talking, offering back to our bodies some of what we gave away in the dancing.

Candace stretches and yawns. "We made a bed for Chloe earlier. We need something for Fiaslet..."

"I'll take care of it," I say. "And the fire. You go on up."

The others head off to their rooms, though Del gives me a considering look on the way out. For now, at least, time is gentle. *The fire is dying down, and night has come.* Not a modern, urgent sort of time, but something we've understood since we first domesticated flame.

"I can sleep on the floor here," says Fiaslet. "Or outside, if it's easier. I am a creature of wild places and passions, you know."

I roll my eyes, but search for the thread of seriousness that I want to articulate. "Hey. So, earlier, when I kissed you—that seemed like it helped. Like something you needed."

I'm still sitting on the floor by the hearth, and they're standing, touching as little as possible in the darkness. A crescent of their cheek reflects the fire's faint orange glow. Now they hold themself even stiller. "I am what I am. I always need that."

"I chose to touch you. It felt like that mattered, but I don't want to assume my instincts are right."

I release a breath as they nod slowly. "It was a gift. That you stopped the mountain from using me as it would, that you touched me willingly against its purposes. I don't get that often. Thank you."

"It didn't keep you from enjoying yourself, that the house could make it safer for me?"

They squat—the deep, heels-down version that you lose if you grow up with chairs everywhere—and cock their head with a trace of amusement that's wonderfully better than the lost, closed look from a minute ago. "I don't have to be a dangerous pleasure to get what I need. And the fact that you're dangerous, too, is not a barrier to enjoyment."

I've never thought of myself as dangerous before. "I don't want to hurt you."

"That would be malice; it's not the same thing as danger. Malice isn't attractive; it's just exhausting. Danger is—" They drop their eyes, and even here in the heart of the house's protection I can tell that they've damped down everything they can. "—enticing."

I lean over and put my hand on their arm. I feel strange, daring, like I've found something long-buried in a drawer, something I've been afraid to look at. A sword, or a dress that used to fit, or—wasn't I going stop trying to put words to these things? Fiaslet is warm and shivering. "So you wouldn't mind if I kept choosing?"

They stay still, but they stop damping down, and I can feel that too, the spill of raw sexual desire through the shield of the hearth's protection. I pull them over me, pull their lips against mine, run fingers through feathery hair, taste smoke and pine and wild mint on their tongue.

"Here?" asks Fiaslet breathlessly, eyes shining more than the embers in the fireplace.

"Hold on." My brain stumbles a moment over the question of whether the fire needs putting out or whether magic overrules the usual safety precautions, and my lack of memory for *how* one puts a fire out, before finally I just press my hand against the wall and think *you mind tucking that away for the night?* and the embers fade to black as I learn that houses can be amused. "Let's go upstairs."

#

The morning sun slips through the loft window and my first thought, waking, is, *Really ought to install blackout curtains, I'm not on a regular schedule any more*. It's a lazy, comfortable idea—something that needs fixing, that can be put on a list to work through at my own pace. I roll away from the light, and into the person sharing my bed. That's a less familiar sensation. My eyes slit open to Fiaslet's back and the tangle of aqua and green fanning over my cheap sheets. They're sleeping still, knees tucked against their chest atop the covers. Fine iridescent hair dusts their legs and arms. A mammal, more or less, though more obviously not-human with their clothes off. Very nicely so, I recall.

They don't snore, either.

My brain is coming back online, and I prod my reactions. I don't feel like I've lost something. Not drained, or desperate. I think of pleasures, pizza and purring cats and late-night kisses, and they all sound appealing. I've never been a turned-on-in-the-morning sort of person, and I'm not now, though still aware of the attraction rolling off Fiaslet in thoughtless waves. I play scenarios: what if they wanted to stay in my room forever, or leave this a one night stand? The first feels a little intrusive and toastery; the second feels sad but not devastating.

The house hovers protectively at the edge of awareness. I'm not facing Fiaslet's temptations with mere human will-power. Which means I can face them, I hope, as a friend, and see what else develops.

Over this sliver of confidence, worry about the coming afternoon creeps like sunlight across the bed. We did *some-thing* last night, but I don't actually understand *what*, or how it will stand up against risks worse than any we faced yester-day. I don't know what might be forced on Fiaslet, or Chloe, or on me and my oldest friends—the people who stuck with me through years of mutual stubborn stupidity, who found me on the other side of those broken years, and who sud-denly share my magic. Even more than the desire to grow something with Fiaslet, I want to explore that magic with Del and Candace. To build with them, at a leisurely pace, this new thing layered over everything we've already done and planned.

I recognize now the sick feeling that my belly has con-jured: the sense of an impending deadline that, even if met, threatens to make the period of its imminence a misery.

Fiaslet's eyes flicker open, settling into a glower at the sunlit window. They roll toward me, away from the light, grunting un-seductively.

"Nocturnal?" I ask, lightly as I can.

They sigh and trace a finger along my bare arm. "Time never demanded my attention, before the mountain." Before I can figure out how to respond, they add, "Thank you."

"My pleasure?" This is my standard as-suave-as-possible response to post-sex compliments, which is not in fact par-ticularly suave. I am not a particularly suave person, which I hope Fiaslet figured out before going to bed with me.

"Not just the sex, though I *am* grateful for that. It's been too long since I've fucked by shared choice, and not by the mountain's will. I feel better than I have for a long time, except—" They hesitate. "I've felt this approaching for years. That I would come to the end of compromising myself for survival, and rebel, and pay the price. You and the Hearth have given me a night between that rebellion and its cost, to brace myself and to lie with the relief and the fear. That is what I thank you for. The shelter before what comes next."

"You're welcome." What else can I say? They would laugh if I suggested that I understand. That I know what it's like to feel a momentous decision bearing down. That there might be something on the other side. "But I hope we can give you more than the one night."

Their focus sharpens, not happily. "The Hearth has power. You are glorious in it." I blink, because there's a hint, in their tone, as if they're the one lying with a creature out of legend. *So which one of you is the hot vampire, and which one is the mortal?* "But the mountain will not permit his contracts to be gainsayed. I have never seen him lose."

I don't want to ask, but I don't know enough to avoid it. "What do you expect him to do?"

Their hand creeps back to their wrist, but I catch it on its way. They smile up at me briefly, wryly. I'm propped on one elbow, so when they rearrange themself to lie on my lap, there's a moment of awkward pillow wrangling and then it feels natural: their head on my legs, hair feather-light against my skin, their legs dangling off the bed. I take their hand again, hoping it makes it easier.

"I honestly don't know," they admit. "We're not exactly a community, the people who owe the mountain. He calls us family, but he wants obedient children, not cousins who love one another. And I'm not someone he sends to punish disobedience."

They fall quiet for a minute, and I give them time. 'I don't know' can reflect real ignorance or a more complicated reluctance, and I'm not surprised when they go on. "He has among his contracts children of the hunt, weakened and bound by his sacrifice of his own earth. They are claw and blood, and go among humans only when ordered. They've never liked me, and they'd welcome the chance to prove my dependence on humans a vulnerability. But he has many humans as well, not only Chloe's parents, but others for whom obedience is well-practiced. Or there are hunters who depend on passing in civilization even more than I do, who've sold themselves for the documentation they now need to live among scholars and soldiers."

"Do they all hate him?"

The wait this time is longer. "I doubt Chloe's parents know him well enough. The others... it's hard to tell. It's not something we admit. Show cracks in your loyalty, and others will use it to gain his favor. I don't think he cares how we really feel about him, but he'd rather we hate each other."

#

We all make our way downstairs slowly. We offer each other tea, french toast, board games. It feels like an election night, after we've put in all the work we can and are waiting on the news—except that we've left NPR off, find ways to avoid our phones. I'm afraid to check social media, because I don't have the bandwidth to handle it if there's been a school shooting today, or if I've somehow missed an ugly case in the Supreme Court. If the mountain turns out to work by Twitter doxing, I'm going to be completely blind-sided. Only Chloe scrolls compulsively, texting friends who don't seem to know the details of her fight with her parents, but who send her memes about Australian wildlife that she shares with forced cheerfulness.

At about 3—I think still too early for our official dead-line—there's a knock on the door. The fire leaps to life. Fiaslet stiffens, and I drop my cards from the resource management game I've been playing badly. I touch the wall, sense readiness and tension.

"Have to offer hospitality and protection, get to break it as soon as they do?" I review the rules, giving myself a needed moment. I can feel my own pulse, ready and tense, and my throat regretting that last slice of French toast.

"If they ask," says Chloe. She puts down her phone. "And no one can hurt us or insult us or make us leave against our wills, as long as we follow the rules."

Fiaslet nods, brushes my wrist in lieu of their own. "And they'll try hard to make us break them."

Candace holds out her knuckles for a fist bump, first with me and then with Del. "Let's go talk to these fuckers very politely."

The whole crowd trails behind me, no point in pretending the mountain doesn't know who's here. But somehow it's me in front now. Me with a house in my head and friends at my back, opening the door to see what's waiting.

My first thought is "bonsai dryad": the twiggy fingers wrapped delicately around a briefcase are all bark and leaves, but clipped close and held in human shape by a tweed business dress and jacket. Their hand, when they hold it out to shake, is tipped with thorns. I start to offer my own, automatically, converting the gesture awkwardly to a bow as I spot the jagged stinging nettle leaves peaking from their sleeves.

"Mia Green," they say. "Hello, Fiaslet."

"Hello, Mia." Fiaslet's voice is neutral. "One of the mountain's hedge lawyers. Not where I would have expected him to start, after yesterday. Aren't you early?"

They don't have a face, precisely. Knots in wood, glints of something bright beneath the surface. Still I get the sense of an amused smile. "I'm trying to forestall the need for anything to happen that one could be early *for*. May I come in?"

I take a steadying breath. "We're the keepers of the Hearth. You're welcome to come in, of course—we're glad to offer our protection, as long as you join in preserving it."

Mia cocks their head. "Perhaps we'd better talk here."

"As long as you understand that the people already under our protection remain so."

"Yes." For a moment their voice is less polished lawyer, more rustling leaves. "I know how the Hearth works."

The porch wraps halfway around the house, bigger than some apartments I've lived in. For now it's mostly a place to stack boxes of gardening supplies. The hedge lawyer pulls over the nearest couple of boxes, pats one to test its structural integrity before sitting down, and lays the briefcase on the other: an impromptu corporate desk suddenly as apparent in the cardboard as the almost-human expressions in the bark above their collar.

I don't sit, though the temptation to do so is strong. Maybe it's only my imagination, but it feels like Mia embodies protocol as much as Fiaslet embodies sex. Feeds off it, perhaps. Maybe I should be more cooperative; whatever comes after the deadline has passed will be worse.

The house growls, and I'm reminded of Chloe and Fiaslet, vulnerable behind me. All inclination to cooperate fades. "What are you here to say?"

"Just this." Mia tilts their head back, unfazed by the need to do so. "You are harboring two people who've violated, or are threatening to violate, contracts with the mountain. That violation comes with penalties that you will be hard pressed to prevent, and other penalties that will fall directly on you if you try. At the same time, enforcing such penalties is obnoxious for the mountain. An unnecessary expenditure of resources."

"That's a shame," puts in Del. "We'll be fine if he decides not to, then."

Candace elbows Del, but Mia repeats their not-quite-smile. "Exactly our hope. We propose a trade: both of the disputed contracts, along with financial considerations—say, five hundred K—in exchange for the deed to this house. You fulfill the obligations you never sought and avoid further risky entanglements, and can purchase a new domicile at far better terms than your loan on this one."

My poker face fails completely. "You're offering to sell us the mountain's ostensible rights over both Chloe and Fiaslet."

"That's right."

"And we could then change the terms of those contracts, or tear them up entirely."

"Correct. Though I do think that would be a waste." Their wooden leer is perfunctory but all-too-expressive.

"In exchange for the Hearth," I say. Which the mountain, of course, could then change the terms on, or tear up entirely. I imagine this refuge, that I'm just learning to be part of, become merely another place where desperate people trade their souls for scraps of safety.

But it would gain us the safety of the only desperate people we've tried to save so far. Chloe could go off to college. Fiaslet would be free. We could get out of this day with none of us dead or injured or bound. And maybe with enough practice and training, we could make another hearth elsewhere and offer the desperate another alternative. The little jagged smile on Mia's face indicates that they know the value of their temptation.

It would be selfishness, pure and simple, to refuse simply because I like who I am here.

I look around at the others, hoping for reprieve. But they all, one way or another, look like they hate the taste of the thing but see the reason in it. Candace is biting her lip, and Del not meeting anyone's eyes. Chloe's fists are clenched, her head bowed. Fiaslet's expression is a painful mix of hope and hopeless fury. They'd get the most out of this. They were expecting to be sacrificed or tortured or both, and surely I owe them a way out. I would owe anyone that, if I could give it to them.

I open my mouth to say something, maybe ask a question to delay the capitulation that already feels inevitable. And I remember: *everyone* involved in a bargain. The house has gone quiet, growls replaced with a quiet, quivering tension. I don't know if it fully understands, or if it can—it's never spoken, only given us the unwavering, opinionated loyalty of a dog. But I wouldn't sell a dog to my worst enemy, regardless of the price.

I pull up a box, lean forward across the "desk." Mine, not Mia's—it's on my porch, after all. "How about all of your contracts?"

"I beg your pardon?" Mia's taken aback, as I intended.

"The hearth is valuable, and has proven its value more thoroughly than two random contracts that the mountain seems eager to foist off. We could save a lot of people over the next couple of decades. If we're giving that up, we'd better get some saving in up front—so we'd want to take over *all* the contracts the mountain currently holds."

I hear Fiaslet's startled laugh behind me, and know I've jumped the right way even as Mia exclaims, "You must be out of your mind! He'd never agree to that!"

I shrug. "How would *you* feel about it?"

They stand, and the desk is boxes again, the lawyerly glare an illusion of branch and leaf. "I want to be on the right side of the fight when he comes to tear the heart out of your walls. Have a good day."

"That's not an answer," I call after them.

"You're out of your mind." And then they're down the driveway and gone.

As I try to decide what to say to everyone else about our dubious life choices, Fiaslet grabs me in a graceless hug and buries their face in the crook of my neck. I wrap my arms around them, feeling strangely unsure. "I'm sorry. I couldn't—"

"Don't apologize," they interrupt, muffled. They lift their head to add, more clearly: "I didn't rebel only for you to surrender."

#

Inside, still unsure exactly what storm we're waiting for, we congregate again around the dining room table.

"I hate to even bring this up," says Candace, fidgeting with her lacy hem, "but should we call the cops? I wouldn't, normally, but we *are* being threatened with serious violence. And if the mountain were willing to let authorities get a good look at magical hit squads, it'd probably have happened by now."

I wrinkle my nose. Yet another logical course of action that just doesn't feel right.

Candace throws up her hands. "I know, but—"

"But Chloe's technically a runaway," Del points out. "So maybe not. Also, he's probably got deals with local police chiefs, just on principle. Probably in a way that looks like mundane corruption to them, but would still result in them not showing up, or sending the one guy who happens to be a werewolf in the mountain's pay, or—"

"Okay, I get it!" Candace rubs her forehead. "Rugby squad?"

"Probably can't actually stand up to these guys."

"Neither can we!"

I whistle sharply. Anxiety spirals, at least, I know how to handle. "Guys, not getting mad at each other for suggestions *or* critiques when a project's due, right?"

Chloe looks up from her nervous origami; a tiny multicolored menagerie already spills over her napkin. "So the thing about calling cops is, it's a way of defining identity. For the whole situation. It collapses your possible solutions to either a standoff or a firefight, neither of which would improve the situation even if they *didn't* notice me."

That's interesting. "Can we define the situation in other ways? Limit what the mountain can do?"

"That's what we did last night."

63

We sing more. Dance a little. Put out snacks and tend the fire in the hearth, with what kindling we can find an easy dash from the house. He has to show up soon, right? Today's thunderstorm is rolling in, heat lightning flickering behind the trees. I can feel the air pressure dropping inside my ears. Something's coming.

A low-pitched roar echoes outside: more mechanical than thunder, or more alive, or both. I look out the window beside the mural, afraid of what I'll see and still taking comfort from the sheltered, sheltering flame. It feels familiar, already, from this past day that's felt more real than most of my adult life: facing danger with the others behind me, ready to find the words I already know how to say.

But I don't know words to describe what I'm facing. The sound was motorcycles, I can see that, the kind that are all shine and bulk and noise and get merged with horses in a certain sort of country song, of course he'd have those. *On* the bikes, dismounting, are less recognizable things. One of them is stone and moss squeezed into human shape. It's flanked by two maybe-women with faces like foxes and tufted ears, grinning at the house and gripping their bike handles with identical taloned hands. And haloing those three, something that swarms like miniscule starlings. As the bike-engine roar fades down, another sound swells, a whining angelic harmony like pressing your ear against a car window on the highway.

The sound gets into my head, makes me think of end-less childhood road trips and the boredom of the familiar. It whispers that the answer to all my problems isn't to stay here, but to throw a few things in a bag and go, go, go. The house's growl cuts through the temptation, but there's pain to the resistance, like forcing myself to work on an article when I'd rather be outside.

"Ugh, what is that thing?" asks Chloe.

"Siren swarm," says Fiaslet. They scratch their arms, wincing. "It doesn't have a name, and I regret to tell you that it's made of mosquitoes. I don't recommend actually going outside."

"Of course he has mosquitoes working for him," says Candace. "Probably fire ants too, I bet. What about the others?"

"Flint, I recognize. He's an old spirit, displaced and then preserved by the mine, like Mia. I've heard of the blood sisters, too. Enough to know that they're here because they want to be."

The swarm's song grows quieter and more piercing. It's prodding, testing, learning; the house struggles to adapt. The rest of the mountain's folk begin prowling around the yard. They, too, seek a break in our defenses. I pace within in parallel, doing what I know how to do. I still have my toolbelt, and as I tap protruding nails, touch up scratched corners, oil hinges, I find myself sharing the house's awareness as yesterday it joined with mine. I *inhabit* like a possessing spirit, knowing pipes and wires in lieu of veins, windows for eyes, shingles that brace like sails under decades of wind and rain. Old, solid, sure of my purpose. And with keepers to share my existence, quick and clever as well as strong and patient. Together we track the small sharp spirits outside, shoring up our joins against them.

Droplets begin to fall, cool and sweet against my walls. It's my work to protect others from the wet and chill, but I myself thrive under them. For my whole existence I've hummed with the shake and boom of thunder, creaked in the wind as comfortably as a willow bends. These attackers are different, not only a threat to fragile flesh but full of malice against *me*. The moss-creature—Flint—flings himself against a crack in my brick foundation. Too late to patch now, I imagine quick-dry cement and the careful movements that will pack it into the gap. My promise holds against the impact; I know with bone-deep, rafter-deep certainty that the attack will reverberate until I keep that promise, ready to break walls and the magic behind them.

I can hear the swarm, but its song falters under the rain's stinging assault. The blood sisters set a glow in the air, keeping fragile bloodsucker wings dry until they dive into the bushes growing rampant around the porch rail. It renews its call from there, while the sisters drag talons across flaking paint. *Sanding and refinishing, I promise. Every plank and column cleaned and varnished.* I sense the sisters' hunger, but also their hesitation. Not creatures of built places, I suspect.

Chloe's arm closes on my human wrist. "Help."

Fiaslet hovers behind her. "She tried to go outside. I held her back. The swarm *will* break her heart; it's what the road does."

Still trying to remember the difference between skin and plaster, I grasp Chloe's hand in return. "You've been wanting to run for a long time, haven't you?"

She nods, still obviously bracing against the pull. "It was going to be college. Now, who knows if I'll get to go anywhere?"

"You'll go wherever you want. But not today, not with that horde waiting for you to step outside. The sisters, I think—they're wild things, they couldn't come into any house, but they wait for the swarm to lure people out. And then they share the blood."

"Uck." The image at least distracts Chloe from claustrophobia. She shakes her head as if movement might clear it. "Does it get to you?" she asks Fiaslet.

"The swarm? It would have to sing a different song. I'm already bound, however far I go, and it hasn't got the power to make me forget that."

I squeeze their hand too, and we head down together to check on the others. They're fine, and I hear them before I see them—as caught up in the Hearth's defense as I've been, at the table singing war songs. Candace breaks off after the final chorus of a rousing Irish call-to-battle for one of several not-worth-it kings. "So are they going to keep poking until we run out of groceries?"

"I don't know," I say, looking to Fiaslet. "Not that I know the mountain well, but siege doesn't seem like his style."

"Not that he's knowable, but it isn't. He'll escalate."

With human eyes, the view through the window is surreally physical. How can a looming stone figure tread across our walk and leave prints in the half-wild flower bed? How can the sisters' foxfire set the yard aglow in flickering oranges and blues? My belief wavers, and in that moment of doubt a car pulls up, ordinary and gray and entirely believable.

"That's him," says Fiaslet. It's unnecessary; the gray man is entirely himself. He pauses with his hand on the car door, frowning up at our house as if at a typo on a tax form. Mia gets out from the shotgun seat, leans casually against the hood. Little vines creep from their wrists across the metal.

The blood sisters return to the gray man. They bow and lick his hands, then slink to opposite sides of the car. They open the back doors and pull out a pair of passengers. "Mom," gasps Chloe. "Dad!" She clings to me harder, a cut-off sob catching in her throat.

They look like people you'd find at a drum circle or a late-night concert in Northampton. Long, loose hair, the woman wearing a gauzy peacock skirt and draping beads, the man with a cheerful red beard and a tunic over leggings. They get out calmly, to all appearances perfectly comfortable with the clawed hands at their wrists. Perfectly unconcerned that their runaway daughter is here, under threat by those same claws.

"They have no protection from the demands of the contract," Fiaslet offers quietly. "They're in thrall."

"If he has them try and talk me out—you can offer them hospitality, right? It would protect them just like it protects us. We'd have time to figure it out." Chloe's voice is urgent, hopeless. "I'm so mad at them."

"They screwed up really badly," I tell her. "But yeah, if we can convince them to accept our hospitality, maybe they'll figure out how to make it up to you." I think of Autumn holidays, the mercy of cool days. "Atone."

But the gray man doesn't send them puppet-like to the porch. They remain by the car, held by twin taloned grips. Twin-like, they tilt their heads, baring necks; Chloe's mom unwraps a scarf from hers. It dangles from her free hand. It's Mia who approaches, their knock that rattles the door while we stare, frozen.

We answer. Of course we do.

"Fifteen minutes," they say, the moment we can hear them. "Chloe and Fiaslet come out and forswear the Hearth's protection. Or your parents pay their share of the contract obligation more swiftly than they can afford." Behind them, the blood sisters place claws against unflinching necks. "They will not resist." They turn without waiting for response, striding back to their master. I close the door numbly.

"Why not demand you come out right away?" It's the only thing I can think of, a stupid question in the face of the threat.

Fiaslet shrugs sadly. "People are braver when they don't have time to think through consequences. He likes to give them just enough time to fear, not enough to think of alternatives. Not that there are any, usually."

Chloe clutches her hand to her mouth, curling in on herself in the middle of the foyer. "I don't want them to *die*. I have to—but *you*—" She stares at Fiaslet. "I can't ask you. You can't—" She doesn't cry, though she looks like she wants to.

"I told you, I have to pay the cost of my rebellion." They grab my hand, kiss it swiftly. "I thank you for the night of reprieve. Again."

It's Del who interrupts. "Fifteen minutes may not be enough time to think of alternatives, but let's try anyway. Organize now, mourn later." With a pointed look, they lead us back to the table.

Ideas we reject as quickly as we think of them: send Chloe and Fiaslet out, but have them fight instead of surrendering. Make a rush together. Call 911 and hope we don't pressure the gray man into anything. I wish one of us had experience with hostage negotiation or something. I vaguely remember reading about how you have to ease pressure on hostage-takers, but I have no idea how to apply that here. And I don't think the gray man feels the stress that a human would in the same situation. He waits outside, unmoving, a mountain that knows everyone will come to it in time.

"When Del got divorced," says Candace slowly, "we did a cord-cutting ritual, to mark that the relationship was truly over. That was symbolic, but could it be real? Could identity magic change who you are, enough to make you no longer your parents' child? And would that make a difference to the contract?"

"I remember that," says Del, and I do too. The look of weightlessness on their face, relief greater than finalizing the paperwork.

Chloe's eyes widen. She shakes her head. "But I *am* their child. Is that really something—I mean, I think you *could*. It would be dangerous to change something so big. But not as dangerous as going outside. I think. Would it—?"

"If you weren't their child..." Fiaslet's ears twitch. They rub their wrist. "The contract hangs on their parental power over you. If you didn't break it, you might well weaken it, enough for them to fight back and you to resist his control. I'm not sure what *else* you would do. It's not a sort of relationship that I've had myself for a long time."

"You'd still be bound, wouldn't you?" Chloe asks. "To do something that might not even be possible any more?"

They bare their neck, mirroring Chloe's parents outside. Their fingers drift to caress their throat. "I wasn't going to do it anyway. I am not planning to escape the consequences."

"Seven minutes," says Candace.

Chloe straightens, rigid with determination. She grabs her bag. "Right."

She kneels in front of the fireplace; flames leap in response. Where we've been singing, hammering, all the most concrete demonstrations of selfhood in service of our newfound magic... Chloe is simply, quietly, obviously herself. Whatever else has brought her relationship with her parents to this point, for a moment I envy her a lifetime of practice in that selfhood. And I wish I could offer her, in return, a sliver of the unexciting, unquestioned love I share with my own parents, with my sister and niece. I owe them calls.

She fumbles for her wallet, pulls out student ID and driver's license. "I call on the world to witness. I am Chloe, but I reject the name of Davis." She throws the IDs on the fire. They melt, spark, burn. "I am not Alice and Jimmy's daughter. I belong only to myself." The words are simple, but I feel it: the witness that makes them more than words. Attention, immanent in the air and the fire, before which even the house checks the straightness of its shingles in respect.

I hold still under the pressure of that attention: a moment, and then it passes like wind from a train that isn't mine. That moment, and then Chloe folds before the fire, sobbing.

I've never been good at saying clever things when people need comfort, so I do my best with the standard noises, with my arm around her heaving shoulders, with the hope that scripts will be enough. "It's all right, shhhh. We've got you."

Between tears, a child's confusion: "How can they be gone? I had them, and now I *don't*. I was so mad, I miss them so much—"

And outside, an answering scream, "Chloe!"

She leaps up, runs to the window—not to the door. I follow, and the others crowd behind us, save for Fiaslet giving cautious space. Outside, Chloe's—what shall I call them? Alice and Jimmy, no longer enthralled, have turned on the blood sisters. A gash runs red down Alice's arm. She and her husband are moving, dancing with the grace and abandon of ravers, and before them the sisters drop to all fours, snarling and clawing but unable to come closer. Flint slows as if in a monster's nightmare. Through the house's perceptions,

70

I sense how the two workers turn their foes' own identities against them, an aikido of definition.

The gray man watches, cold fury in his face. But he does nothing to aid his minions.

"Should we… ask them in?" suggests Candace uncertainly.

Chloe's face is streaked with tears. "I don't know," she whispers.

I watch them, focused in their movements as T'ai Chi masters. "Let's give them a moment."

The gray man's glare sweeps the yard, then rises to our window. I try not to shrink. I can guess Fiaslet's terror, and the best I can do is stand in the way and glare back. He can't win now, but he can be a poor loser. He can still punish defiance.

Fiaslet wraps their arms around me from behind. Their touch remains intoxicating, even under the circumstances; I turn around without thinking. They bend to kiss me, lips sweet as mead and lilacs. Then they pull back. "I need to go out now."

"What? No!"

Del piles on. "Why? He threatened Chloe's—whatever they are now—but he can't follow through any more."

"Stay here," urges Candace. "We'll protect you. We thought of something for Chloe, we'll figure it out for you too."

They shake their head, feathery hair rustling. "Chloe has magic that I don't. And I told you, I knew there would be a price for my rebellion. Now he can't make me hurt anyone else when I pay it."

"He can hurt *you*," I point out. "He could kill you."

"He will, I expect. I've lost my utility. But I can't stay in your house forever—that would just be another prison, even with more pleasant company." They touch my cheek, too briefly. "I shouldn't ever wish to find you, or your holy place, stifling. I cannot get back the life that fit my nature, and I would rather die than hurt you by struggling against the constraints of the Hearth's hospitality."

They pull away, striding toward the door. I hurry after them: angry, desperate, yelling to keep the argument going. "Don't talk like that! Wait—just give it a fucking moment, your martyrdom is not that fucking urgent! Give us a chance to be something—"

Something other than a cage. Something other than proof that safety just holds you back.

The mountain's anger weighs on the air outside, like the pressure change before a hurricane.

I think as I talk, or talk as I think. If I stop talking they'll leave, and be gone forever. "You said Chloe has power you don't. That humans force others' identities. But it doesn't need to be force." Faster, as ideas come. "We could make the change for you, whatever you asked! You could tell us what you want to be, and we could do the magic. Something just different enough to break your contract. Please, Fiaslet, let us try!"

It holds them from the door, at least. "I've had too much change forced on me already. I've lived too far beyond the point when I could be myself."

"So between change or die, you'll pick *die*? Without even taking an hour to think about it?"

They don't turn around. "I've been thinking about it for a long time."

I'm frozen, furious. It's Chloe who pulls them around, grabbing their arm when before she didn't dare touch them. "You're scared! I just gave up having parents, who were frustrating and overprotective and stifling and *mine*, and who were part of every plan I had for my life, to get out of this. I changed my whole life and I had *fifteen minutes* to think about it. I don't want *you* because neither of us had a choice and you aren't my fucking type, no offense, but—" She takes a breath. "You are fabulous and dangerous, and the world would be worse without you in it. You cared enough

72

about giving me a choice to die for it, and the world would be worse without that, too. We're stuck with a world that has that asshole out there, and we deserve to have *you* too. You deserve to survive and spite him and help people fight him, even if it's harder and scarier. So put on your big girl pants and help us figure out how to make that happen."

Fiaslet tenses, but doesn't pull away from Chloe. And finally, after a long moment, they turn around.

"Not tame," they say. "I won't survive as anything tame."

My heart swells, and something behind my heart, too. "Not tame. But maybe differently dangerous?"

The smile that breaks through is painful: Fiaslet's own desire, deeper than hunger or lust. Chloe draws back, giving them space to want. They close their eyes and stretch their fingers as if grasping something. "Oh. Yes. I want all the danger I haven't been allowed to be since I dealt for my safety. I want my kiss to terrify people with their freedom, with their wildest and truest selves. I want to draw their power to the surface, no matter how inconvenient it is for—" Their eyes flick open, purple as the core of a flame, and they glance at the door. "—that. To leave lovers in danger because they *won't* deal any more."

I'm shivering with delight and fear, and the house's own eagerness. Before, it was protecting Fiaslet, and protecting me from their magic. Now it wants them itself. I step back to the space before the leaping flame, where a just minutes ago Chloe made herself an orphan, and beckon. "We can do that. You already started, by coming here in the first place."

Fiaslet's bright eyes brighten. Quick strides bring them close enough that I can feel their heat mixing with the fire. I wrap my arms around their shoulders, drawing them into a kiss that comes as much from the Hearth as from me. It's hot enough to burn, sweet enough to make the burning worth it. When they pull back, I see where my fingers have marked their skin. Like the first time when I opened the door to Chloe's knock, the words come through me. "We offered the house's protection, as you joined in providing it. Now we offer you a place as a keeper of a different sort. Give up what you have served elsewhere, and give strength where our shelter cannot protect. Be our—" and here the house, used to working with those who live within its walls, frustrated by all the prisoned folk who never come here for help, pauses to seek words. I find one: "—knight."

Fiaslet touches their shoulders, wincing at the burns left by my hands, lips parted in wonder. They kneel, looking up. "I accept your offer. I will change, and be a knight of the hearth." And then gasps, bent double for a heart-wrenching second in pain, or shock. But before I can react, they sit up again, shaking, offering their wrists for me to examine. Of any mark or metal, only scattered glints remain.

I hear the gray man shouting outside, his cool façade cracked. I grin at Fiaslet with the house's righteous fury. "Shall we show them?"

"I—" Fiaslet's attempt at speech transmutes into a groan as they fall back to hands and knees, gasping. Magenta, not quite the shade of human blood, wells against their shirt.

"Shit! Candace, where the fuck did we pack the first aid kit?" She dashes upstairs while Del and I lay Fiaslet before the hearth; Chloe appears a moment later with the blanket from her impromptu bed. Del struggles with their lent-out shirt, swears, and gets scissors to cut it off. Bared, Fiaslet's chest is a mass of scored lines. They're bleeding less than I expected, but they're puffy and red: clearly infected, possibly worse if there's some sort of poison involved.

Candace comes back. "Fuck. That doesn't look great." She pulls out gauze and rubbing alcohol, starts cleaning the wounds as best she can. Fiaslet whimpers and writhes. "I don't suppose they told you anything last night about the exact nature of their injuries?"

I shake my head. I press the back of my hand against their temple. "Feverish. Or at least hotter than, um, than they were. Would acetaminophen work, do you think?"

Candace glances at Del, who frowns. "Um. If I remember right from my ag med colleagues, that's only okay for humans, and I don't know how human they are. Ibuprofen's probably safer."

We manage to get a couple pills into them, and Candace slathers their chest with triple antibiotic ointment and starts on bandages. I can feel the house trying to help, but healing century-old wounds is a bit beyond its remit. On the other hand, we have things in our first aid kit that no one had a century ago. Maybe it'll be enough.

It'd be nice if this were the only remaining danger. I don't want to leave Fiaslet, but I get up anyway. I step onto the porch with the Hearth's power blazing behind my glare. The house is as eager to be of use as I am, as angry at the power that forced this.

The gray man is leaning over the hood of the car, breathing hard. His people are on one side with him, Alice and Jimmy on the other. I hoped I'd see his own suit blood-stained—but however much backlash has hit him, he can diffuse it a lot further. And whatever of Fiaslet's injury has stayed with Fiaslet, it occurs to me suddenly, is stolen forever from the mountain's armory. Mixed blessings. Somewhere in our bushes the siren swarm whines, ignorable and dissatisfied.

"Mountain!" I shout to be heard over the rain. "We don't have anything of yours now! You've got nothing left to gain here!"

Alice calls back, before the gray man can say anything. "Chloe! What happened to Chloe?"

"Wait your damn turn!" I tell her. The mountain is at the far end of a long chain of bad life choices; Alice and Jimmy could've prevented this whole thing just by being better people this week. "You brought this on your own damn self."

The gray man straightens, effort more obvious than I suspect he'd like. "What. Did. You. Do?"

I consider not telling him, then consider that his minions are right here. "Fiaslet and Chloe are no longer the people who contracted with you. They've chosen to become something else. And any of your remaining..." I recall the word he used. "...*vassals* are welcome to do the same. Or you can go now, and try to convince them that you're worth serving when they have a choice." The blood sisters glare, but I see something change in how Flint stands. I hope he's listening.

Mist thickens around the gray man, the lie of his human form slipping. "Steal from me again, and I'll burn you to the ground."

I flinch inwardly, but we were always going to come away from this conversation with an enemy. "Stealing would mean we have something of yours. We don't, even by your rules." *Take the pressure off.* "Neither of us has anything more to gain from fighting today. We can work out our long-term disagreements another time."

I don't know if that actually counts as taking the pressure off or not, but the gray man snarls at his people and gets in the car. The swarm lifts and settles itself in the safe glow of the blood sisters' shoulders, and they rev their bikes and follow their master. Flint looks back, head shifting ponderously, and I wonder if he's going to stay and talk. But no, not today. He turns and follows the others.

That leaves Alice and Jimmy. They make their sodden way to the porch.

"May we come in?" asks Jimmy. The events of the past hour seem to have sobered them a bit.

"Of course you can come in," I say. "The Hearth doesn't turn anyone away. But I'm not sure if you want to."

"I know we screwed up," says Alice. "We just want to talk to her. Apologize, for a start. We should never have tried to get anything good out of—that. Him."

I shake my head. "She's in there right now, mourning you. Because breaking any connection you could've fixed was the only way to keep you safe, and make her safe from the mess you made. So what's it going to do to her if you try to fix something that isn't there any more? Or what would happen if you somehow succeeded—would your contract resurrect itself too?"

Jimmy draws himself up. "But she's our daughter!"

"Not any more. I'm sorry. If she were, you could never have fought back."

Alice puts her hand on his arm, restraining further argument. "Let's go home and talk about it. We know she's safe here, and we need to figure out what she's done. If there's any way to undo what she—sacrificed—without undoing what she saved. The worst thing we can do is go off half-cocked again." She looks up at me from the bottom of the steps. "Tell her—whenever she's ready to call. Tell her we're working on it."

"I will." But unless she asks, maybe not today.

#

Inside, Fiaslet curls on the blanket in front of the fire, shivering. But they seem to be breathing more easily. They shift awkwardly to peer at me through slitted eyes. "Candace says... antibiotics?"

I nod and sit next to them on the floor, stroking their side as they get comfortable again. "No poisons or anything? Just infected?"

"Already been through that checklist," says Candace. "I think they're going to be okay."

#

A week later, we're sitting around the kitchen table. We've been doing that a lot, in between unpacking and finishing the doorknobs and scrounging up concrete to mend that crack. Sitting at the table, keeping each other company. Looking after Fiaslet, now recovering on a somewhat more comfortable pallet by the fire; the house had strong opinions about moving them elsewhere. Eating. Talking. Breathing. Planning a future, or maybe—one of those administrative buzzwords from which you can occasionally drill through to a true heart—envisioning one.

Chloe's still crashing on our air mattress, planning out a gap year and an unexpected new life. I'm wondering if she might make another knight for the Hearth, once she's had enough breathing time that I won't feel pushy asking. For now, she's teaching us, more 101 lessons for our own unexpected future.

The gray man hasn't come back yet. None of us have tried to drive over the Notch, either.

Fiaslet's sitting up at last, shaky, but awake and lucid. Stress-borne pheromones roll off their body. The flavor's different, though: still brain-bendingly alluring behind the Hearth's shield, but now it makes *me* feel dangerous. Eager. I'm not used to feeling this ready for the unknown, but I welcome it.

"I could offer art classes at local shelters," Del suggests. "Bring in something for utilities, and keep an eye out for people who need our kind of help."

"I'm not sure that pays, technically," says Candace. "Then again, my best idea is to try and get that Storys'n'Sewing podcast off the ground. Bohemia may not be dead, but it's probably broke. Or I can ask my folks for a loan." Chloe throws an origami star at her, as requested earlier. It's good to have backup options from people who have actual money, but none of us are there yet.

Chloe starts work on another star. "I told you, it's not prosperity gospel bullshit. Magic won't ever make you rich, but it'll make sure you have *enough*. Just barely."

"We can deal with enough," I tell her. I tilt my chair back, taking in the heat of the day and of the fire, feeling again that sense of eager possibility that I don't yet understand, and don't actually need to understand. "As long as we can *do* this. As long as we can get people coming to the Hearth again. It sounds like it's been a while."

Chloe shrugs. "Everyone knows it's here. But I always got the impression it was a last resort."

Fiaslet's voice is weak but no longer hoarse. "The mountain. He discouraged it. He's good at shaping... how people think. Advertising."

"And spreading nasty rumors about his competition, I bet," adds Candace.

The corners of my mouth draw up, hungry for the fight. "That'll get worse, now that we're actually competing. We need more people ourselves. Not just folks who pass through, like you said they used to, but people who will speak for the Hearth afterwards, or do things farther away than the house itself can reach."

We talk more, throwing out ideas, figuring out how to be better at what we want to become. The topic is urgent but the conversation feels unhurried. We're not on anyone's schedule: we're building something solid, something where the relationships are as important as what we do with them. We stop sometimes to sing or bake or draw visions, and through the open window an evening breeze slips in with the whiff of drying leaves.

There's a knock at the door.

As I go to get it, I realize that I'm never again going to expect that sound to herald Jehovah's Witnesses, or Girl Scouts, or a neighbor complaining about an overgrown yard. Anything could be on the other side, ready to turn our lives inside out. I don't mind the possibility.

What's actually there, when I open the door, is granite and moss shaped almost to human form. On a Berkshire outcrop, he'd fade to perfect camouflage; on our porch he seems to have his own gravity field. Why is he back? Is the mountain trying to threaten us again, pressure us into some-thing?

"My name is Flint." His voice is sandpaper and thunder. "I ask the protection of the House."

I feel again the tug of my lips into that hungry smile. And I think: there is so much power in letting people know they have alternatives. It saved me; it can save you too.

"We offer the house's protection," I promise, "As you join in providing it."

Walking a Wounded Land

Andrew Knighton

WALKING A WOUNDED LAND

To Elmo, who walked with me when I most
needed company.

ANDREW KNIGHTON

WALKING A WOUNDED LAND

Chapter One

To my left is the sea, endlessly in motion, a vast expanse in which my magic has no power. The sea holds no memories, no paths I can walk. To travel the sea, you have to take ship, to place a barrier between yourself and the world. For me, it's a power that matters only because of how it shapes the land.

To my right is that land; stillness and solidity, a place that can hold history. It's already put the first scuffs on my new boots, and now it invites me to continue, to follow trails laid down by those who walked before me. With a wriggle of my shoulders I settle my pack, then check the strap on my camera and set off along the cliff top trail.

The warmth of sunshine on my skin soothes me. I've felt tense since getting off the train at Aldkey, worrying that someone might recognise me, leading to awkward conversations about where I've been for the past few years, or worse still, about the good old days of youth. Those days weren't all that good, and I don't want to make them new again. The further I walk along the cliff top, the less likely that conversation becomes. Only two sorts of people follow this trail: teenagers and tourists, none of whom will know me. Without the anxiety of expectation, I find my stride and I find myself, enjoying a simple, steady rhythm. My body is occupied but not busy, my mind drifting but not distracted. As thoughts fade, I feel the dirt beneath my feet, the rocks below, the grass on the hillside and the windswept trees, their roots reaching into the earth. The essence of the land rises into me, and my essence sinks into it. Call it magic, ghosts, or the memory of the land, it's all the same thing, a piece of your past that you leave for those who follow, and who know how to look. With these footsteps, I carve a trail into the skin of England. Footsteps remain forever, if you know how to find them.

Those footsteps flow through me, echoing down the years, and we walk together. Two walkers appear as shimmering visions on the path. Their steps sway, shaped by long years on the deck of a boat, amplified by a long day of drinking, a wake at the next village for a fisherman lost at sea. Cheering his name, they take their last swigs from a clay jug, then cast it off the cliff.

Another walker appears, sandals slapping. A merchant, come to Britannia with arms for the legions, curious about this legendarily wild land. Separated by centuries of erosion, his coast is miles away from him to the north, but he still pulls his tunic tight against a chill wind, a tourist before there were tourists.

A more familiar vision next, a pair of teenagers, and I know this memory can't be more than fifteen years old, because I know when I got that t-shirt. Me and Ben, back when he was something more than an untouched number in my phone. It hurts to see those smiles, so I brush the image away before I see or hear any more, look for something older, something like...

A young man and a young woman, walking hand in hand. He's wearing a uniform: new boots, khaki jacket, peaked cap. Only two months after arriving at the local barracks, he's already being sent to the mud and blood of Flanders. She squeezes his hand, holding tight to love and fighting the dread of loss. He's anxious, but doesn't want it to show, wants her to remember him well.

The couple step off the path and stop beside a rock, where he pulls out a pocket knife and starts to slowly, carefully scrape their initials into the stone. Pulling back a root and brushing away moss, I find those same letters a century later.

I raise my camera, carefully adjust the focus and light settings, press the button. Click click click. A swift series of digital impressions, a screen-thin imitation of a solid landscape. I'll look up those initials later, find his name in the regiment's records, maybe even work out who she was. These small details bring a story to life, let me make a living off guidebooks and blog posts. Though our magic is a secret, plenty of walkers find ways to make it useful, to avoid being caged in an office or shop.

As I step back, the couple fade and a new ghost appears. It's the woman again, alone this time, running her fingers over those stone letters as tears run down her cheeks. One more part of the story. I step away. I can't offer comfort to a memory, but I can give her privacy in her grief.

On the cliff path again, I keep heading east, taking photos and notes as I go, letting the ghosts guide me. Stopping on a rise where brambles crawl their barbed way through ferns, I wait, camera in hand, for the brightly coloured coats of hikers to disappear from sight. The view here is spectacular, the waves breaking against a headland, gulls soaring above a stack of stone, a lone tree against the blue sky. A hovering kite adds a note of drama. The people who buy my guides don't want the reality, with other people walking these trails. They want the unspoilt dream.

The hikers disappear over the headland. I take my photos, then walk on.

My pocket vibrates. I unzip it, take out my phone. It's Lynn calling, all the way from Vienna. Weird. We're messaging friends, not phone call ones. It's quite a coincidence, her calling when I'm back home.

I tap the screen, curious at what this could be about. The kite folds in its wings and dives, plummeting onto unseen prey.

"Hi Lynn, what's up? Did you butt dial me from Europe?"

"I'm sorry, Paul, but I'm calling with bad news." Her voice is raspy, hesitant. "Ben died."

The words stop me in my tracks. They're like something out of a story, sounds that hang useless in the air, signifying nothing at all. They can't connect to reality.

"Paul, are you there?" Lynn's voice sounds thick like oil, like it's choking her. That's all she is right now, a voice on the phone. The real Lynn is so far away I can't count the footsteps.

Beneath me, at the base of the cliff, waves crash across stones. The dark sea rips at the pale flesh of the land. Some day, that darkness will win, the cliff will fall, this path where I stand will be gone. But surely not today.

"Paul? Please, say something."

The waves have me hypnotised, watching them wash back and forth. Or perhaps I've hypnotised myself, detached from thoughts that crash and rage as wildly as the waves, thoughts that will destroy me if I step into them, words that will suck me under.

"I don't understand." It sounds stupid, but it's the best I can manage, a way to break through the roadblock in my mind, to step forward into the next moment.

"He..." Lynn takes a deep breath. "Oh, God. Look, I don't have a lot of details. A hiker found him, out on one of the little trails near Multhorpe. Hangman's Hill, I think. It looks like he had a heart attack."

I clutch the phone to the side of my head, fingers squeezing the plastic case. Its hard contours separate me from the workings of the device, from the voice of a friend, from the man I was a moment before, but at least it's something solid, something I can cling to.

"That doesn't make sense." I sink to the ground, leaning back into brambles and ferns. The contents of my pack dig into my back: water bottle, notebooks, a plastic tub. Things that have no place in this natural world. "He's twenty-eight. People don't die of heart attacks when they're twenty-eight."

"I don't know. That's just what I heard."

"It can't be. It doesn't make sense."

"Sometimes the world doesn't make sense, Paul."

"No, but... It can't be."

Lynn's sobbing. I can hear it down the line. I can hear her trying not to, trying to hold herself together. She knew Ben and I when we were at school, she knows how much we meant to each other back then. She's trying to hold herself together for me, and I don't know how to deal with that, because I don't even know what I'm feeling.

"When is... What is..." I pause, try to gather my thoughts. It's like snatching at snowflakes on the wind, most of them fly from my grasp and those I catch melt away before I can see their shape. I feel like I should know what to do, what to say, but there's no template for grief, no class that taught me how to deal with this gaping hole that's been torn in my chest. If I look at that wound, I'm going to bleed out, so instead I stare at the sky, watch the gulls soar and drift, try to picture a future that makes no sense. In the end, I have to ask. "What happens next?"

"I'm not sure. He wasn't with anyone at the moment, so I guess his parents will deal with the funeral."

I nod, though she can't see me. Of course Ben was alone. He stopped having space in his life for other people years ago.

No. That's the bitterness talking. I know better than anyone how warm Ben could be, how much love he had for his friends and family, even if his obsessions ripped him away.

"Perhaps you could give them a call?" Lynn says.

"What?" I've gone blank again. Words are just sounds, out of step with meaning.

"His parents. You knew them better than I did. Perhaps you could call and find out what's happening?"

I hesitate. It's a long time since I've seen Cerys and Dom, and it wasn't a comfortable meeting. He tried to make conversation, but she could barely find two words for me. Hardly surprising, after what happened between me and their son. Still, Lynn's right. I know them. I owe them. I can hardly ignore them in the midst of this.

"I'll go see them. I'm in town this week."

"Really? That's one hell of a coincidence."

It isn't. I see that now. It was an uphill struggle to find my next project, until the invitation came for this book, and I'd accepted it far more easily than I should have done. The magic of paths is one of connections, of threading together the fragments of our lives and of our world. Each footstep is a stitch and the walker is the needle as often as they are the seamstress's hand. The land had known that something was coming, and it brought me back. I don't object; walkers understand better than anyone what we owe the land.

"I'll give you a call," I say, "once I know more."

"Thanks. That would be good." A long silence, then Lynn finds her voice again. "I'm really sorry, Paul."

"Me too."

After we hang up, I sit for a long time staring out at the sea, that vast and dark and merciless expanse. Then I force myself to my feet and start walking west, back towards town. I'm still clutching my phone, a talisman against the chaos, a reminder that all of this is real. If I let it go, I might lose myself.

Ben had been fighting for Multhorpe for years, trying to preserve that part of the landscape in the face of developers. I'd seen news about this obscure local struggle and the nationally known campaigner committing himself to it. The news talked about petitions, court cases, and boundary disputes. Most people didn't know that the power of pathways and boundaries had as much influence over their lives as politics or economics, the other invisible forces running through our every moment. Most people didn't know the real Ben. They wouldn't understand that, if he died out walking, it wasn't just walking. He was doing something deeper and more powerful, something that drew more from him than he could live without. Maybe he really did have a heart attack, but sure as the ocean, something else caused it.

My pace quickens in line with my mood. Other walkers emerge from the air to join me. The grieving soldier's girl, gritting her teeth as she thinks of the war. The sailors from the wake, cursing the waves. A limping smuggler, stained with the blood of a customs agent.

And then one that knocks the breath out of me.

The memories we call ghosts can linger in the land as strongly after two days as two thousand years. Emotion is what matters, human spirits carving the earth like a chisel carves stone, our passions both the sculptor and the shape they leave. Centuries of strangers have marked this trail with traces of themselves, but so have my friends. So have I.

I see a younger me and Ben, stiff backed and swift striding, forced together by a favour for another friend, though the wound's still raw from our argument the week before.

"Just because you don't give a shit about anything," he hisses.

"Just because you don't give a shit about anyone," the ghost of me snaps back.

It's as much as I can stand. I slow my pace and those visions vanish, replaced by others with a slower pace. A Victorian birdwatcher. A wartime observer. A medieval hunter and his dog. My sight blurs as I stumble along the path.

Somewhere in my heart, I had always assumed that Ben and I would find each other again, that the terse, practical messages we occasionally exchange would become the seeds of something more; if not the full bloom of our friendship, then at least something green with life. That possibility has been severed with an insurmountable finality. I didn't know that I was anchored to him until the tide swept him away.

Something wet touches my hand. The hunter's dog. Far more real than any of these other ghosts. Of course he is. What could be more timeless than man's best friend?

No. That's not how the magic works. This is a real dog, here and now, and he's stopped me, right at the edge of the cliff. I swallow hard, put my hand on his head, take a trembling step away from the crumbling edge.

"Oh, thank goodness." A grey-haired woman is rushing up to me, a dog lead in her hand. There's a man behind her. They're both wearing practical, brightly coloured jackets. "We saw you veer across the path, we were worried you would fall off the edge. Are you all right? Have you hurt yourself?"

I can't look at her, so instead I crouch beside the dog. He's a border collie, black with white legs and belly, a pale stripe running down the middle of his face. His ears are raised, tail swishing from side to side, innocent and eager to meet someone new. He licks my hand, tips his head on one side, those big empathetic eyes asking the same question as his owner, and I burst into tears. My whole body shakes as I run a hand down soft fur. He leans in, rests his head on my shoulder. I wrap my arms around him and let the grief flow.

"It's all right." The woman says softly, laying a hand on my shoulder. "It's all going to be all right."

It isn't. I can never apologise to Ben, never heal the rift between us. I can never make up for the things I said.

But perhaps I can do one last thing for him. I can find out what happened. I can show the world who Ben really was.

Chapter Two

I've never been sure where the edge of Aldkey is, where the countryside ends and the town begins. It's the sort of question that seems practical when you first look at it, but that becomes nebulous, philosophical, and uncertain as you stare. In a way, that's a good thing. The magic of borders cuts the land apart, splitting it up and grabbing a piece, while the magic of paths stitches it together, connecting one landmark to the next, making them whole. If there's a place called England, then paths made it, and borders cut it off from the world. If there's a place called Aldkey, then the same rule goes there.

Perhaps that's why we were so fascinated by the boundary when we were younger, why we were discussing it one summer night as we walked home. I walk that same route now, past the town sign and the speed limit, an abandoned garage and a corner shop that might still be open despite its grubby windows. As I take the insouciant pace of a teenager, in no rush to get home, I'm joined by the ghosts of those days. Me and Ben and Star, ambling along, chewing gum, watching the cars rush past.

"Technically, the town ends at that sign," Ben says. "That's the boundary of the electoral district."

Of course he had a clear cut view, and of course it was politically defined. Ben knew who he was better than I did, even back then.

"What about those houses?" Younger me points back the way we've just come. "Surely they're part of the town?"

"Technically, no."

"Then your technicality is nonsense."

It's the sort of statement that could only sound profound at sixteen, but the three ghostly figures treat it with deep significance.

"Where do you think it ends, then?" Ben rubs a finger along the scar that splits his left eyebrow, a sure sign that he considers this serious business.

"Past the houses. You've got to include all the people."

"What do you think, Star? Where's the boundary?"

She's been walking a few feet behind us, but now she stops, spits her gum onto the pavement, uses the toe of her bright green Doc Martens to drag it into a lumpy line.

"Town ends here," she says, then grabs a stick and lays it down a meter further along the path. "Or here. Or at this crack. Or under your sign. Or after your houses. Or at the sea. Or up my ass."

Ben and I laugh, mostly with her, and a little at the way she speaks. Not her Middle Eastern accent, but the Americanisms she picked up learning English off TV.

"I have been stopped at enough borders in my life." She picks up the stick, carries on down the street, swinging it like a baton. "This one will move with me."

The ghost of Star walks through tourists crowding the pavement here and now. I jink left and right, trying to weave my way through. That broken rhythm and the tourists' chatter breaks the trance I've been in, and the teenage ghosts fade away. When I get out the far side, it's just me, walking alone into town, looking for the Star of today.

I find a new rhythm, not the clear confidence of a rural hike but slower, skulking movements, shoulders drawn in, feet barely leaving the paving stones. Magic is all about landscape, and Aldkey isn't the sort of place that strides proudly. Maybe once, when it had factories and more than half a dozen boats sailing out to fish, but the ghosts that match my movements are huddled, tired, uncertain. A labourer from the 1980s, let go by the cannery, an unemployment payment clutched in his fist. An elderly shopper stop-starting past discount stores and charity shops, counting the pennies before she shuffles on. A Victorian tourist, wobbling half-drunk through the middle of the afternoon, anticipating the joys of

a pier that's since been swept away. Once upon a time, Aldkey was the centre of its own little universe, but these days
it's like most small English towns, cringing and clinging on in
the face of a cruel world.

The broken spirit of the town flows through my feet,
and I know straight away that Star doesn't want to be found.
She's scattered her magic, left a trail designed to baffle and
mislead. Hiding from the public eye is a perverse position
for an artist, but that's Star for you. When we were teenagers, Ben and I could keep our outsider status folded away in
the closet. Star didn't have that choice, as one of only seven
brown faces in town, with four of the others her family.
Instead of muffling her identity, she emphasised it, put on an
exaggerated accent, invented strange customs and blamed
them on her homeland, left her persecutors bewildered by a
victim who wouldn't cower. Whatever people wanted her to
do, she wouldn't do it.

She's definitely still in Aldkey. There aren't many people
in the world who know what walking does, let alone how
to use its power, and to my eyes, the streets are marked as
much by the traces of her magic as by the brightness of her
art. An advertising board defaced with situationist slogans
just this side of obscenity. A beautiful mural of a woodland
sprayed onto the end of a derelict factory. Tiny portraits
painted on discs of gum on the pavement, tribute to a London artist she read about years ago, Star defying tradition
by creating a new one. And between them, ghostly images of
her, walking strange rhythms to ensure that they remain.

I follow a twisting, turning route through the streets,
trying to follow the thread of her. It's made more difficult by
people walking this way and that, bumping into each other,
stopping to stare into shop windows or to wait at crossings
for the green man. I switch my pace to match tourists or
locals, different memories emerging with different movements. For some this town is the daily grind, swift footsteps
carrying them through regular routines. For others, its a

place of escape and diversion, of pausing to read a menu or point at a brightly painted boat, then hurrying on to the amusement arcades. Lives lived in a single space but parallel worlds. Through that space run the cars, severing one side of the street from the other, breaking the rhythm of humanity. So close together, we should all be connected, but instead the town is fractured, opaque, like a windscreen in the aftermath of a crash.

Star has hidden herself in this. Every time I find enough rhythm to dip into memory, I see an image of her and I'm drawn to follow it. Every time, that image turns around and pulls a face before disappearing, or vanishes into an older ghost. These aren't clues, they're thumb tacks scattered across the floor, and picking my way through them puts me in a prickly mood.

In principle, I should like urban walking. Its stuttering shuffle and stop-start strides can become a promenade at the boundary of a park or break into riot at a junction. I took part in demonstrations during my year in London, and though I was there for the politics, it was the magic that really hit me, the power provided by thousands of people walking in unison, carving a single purpose into the psyche of the city. If I could have controlled that power, I could have changed the world, though it would be as easy to hold the waves from crashing against the cliffs. It felt like something we should be steering into, those of us who know magic.

But in practice, I don't like towns. You don't get sociable strolls and purposeful parading. You get the endless repetition of tedious routines, back and forth along the same route to work day after day, grinding a meaningless memory into the ground. And worse than that, the fog of shopping, walking not to experience or to create but to accumulate.

I'm caught on that thought as I enter the market square. With a Victorian town hall at one end and a medieval church at the other, it's the only place in Aldkey that ever came close to the grandeur of the countryside, of tapping into something vast and timeless. Of course, it's been ruined by identikit chain outlets and coffee shops, each one with its legally distinct and plastically specific design work. Every shop in the high street is different, every high street in the country the same, and Aldkey has caught that plague.

Familiar anger bubbles in me, protective of a place that offered me no protection, a town I cared about just because it was mine. Stomping across the square, I'm not surprised to find myself accompanied by teenage memory: Ben and I ranting about the replacement of the Old Wagon Wheel with a chain pub while Star throws her head back in a mocking impression of our moans. Another memory of Star, an adult now, watches them, then looks at me, winks, and vanishes. I grit my teeth, but I almost laugh too. She's frustrating, like always, but no one can craft memory as playfully as her.

There's an advertising hoarding at the end of the street, celebrating the latest development from Rackham Enterprises. Steven Rackham, Aldkey's embodiment of inherited privilege, smiles down smugly from next to a picture of a multi-storey car park. They're going to tear down the old theatre for this thing, replace a monument to passion with an ugly concrete box that encourages people to detach themselves from the world and drive that last mile into town, to snarl up these narrow streets. For all its problems, Aldkey used to have small town charm, distinctive shops and tiny landmarks. What's happening to the place I grew up?

Passers by are picking up my angry stride and ugly emotions. I stop, take a deep breath, calm my own mind and then push that calm from me into the ground. Those other people don't get any calmer, but at least no one else is getting mad. I've been channelling my power a lot today, and it's tiring me out, making me careless. Most people can't work magic, and they won't know to resist it. I should rest before I hurt myself or, far worse, someone else.

A connection to the land is a powerful thing, especially in a place where I'm so deeply connected. I still need to find

95

Star, not just because she might know about Ben, but to anchor me here, to help me manage the memories. I should try going somewhere that mattered to us both. The Bell Hotel is nearby, not a perfect choice but a starting place.

I round the corner and a memory rises from the cobbles, so hard and fast it almost knocks me off my feet. A crowd of ghosts outside the pub, a gang of us from sixth form, drinking lager on a summer's evening. It's the first time I've successfully been served in a bar, a moment for celebration, but joy turns sour as Star emerges, followed by a couple of guys with slicked back hair and polo shirts. They're calling her names, the sort of filthy, racist language I've seldom heard before, the sort that curdles your mind as you realise how grotesque human beings can be. She's playing along like usual, telling them how right they are, trying to get away, but their grins only grow more feral. She's changed her voice, changed her clothes, changed the name she goes by, but nothing is ever enough. One of them pushes her, her drink goes flying, she falls.

Ben and I leap up in an instant. He charges, shouting at the men, waving his fists in righteous fury. I dash towards the door, to fetch a bouncer or a barman, some figure of authority. Is it cowardice when you think it might work best? Was I never willing to take a risk?

That younger me dashes through a doorway, but here and now the door is boarded over. There's not even a coffee shop in its place, no for sale sign, no tooth-grinding promise of a new Rackham development. If the old Bell Hotel has a future, its shuttered windows won't tell me what that is.

The ghosts flicker, fade, are gone. As in the town square, all that's left is an older version of Star, dressed in an oversized red shirt and brightly patterned trousers, watching me with a knowing smile. She winks and light ripples off of her, making the air shimmer, but when that passes she remains.

"Are you really here?" I ask. "Now, at the same time as me?"

"Do you want me to be?" Her accent's softened. Perhaps she doesn't need to control it anymore. She's acclaimed, in certain specific circles. She doesn't need to mark herself out for publicity purposes or to hide herself for safety's sake.

Except that she does. The world gets better, but it never entirely casts off the darkness, and she's the sort of bright light that will always stand out.

"Can't you give me a straight answer?" I almost got caught in a labyrinth once, one of those puzzle paths designed to trap an unwary walker, to keep them circling through memories until they fade into a ghost. Sometimes Star's words feel like a labyrinth for the mind, and I struggle to keep my frustration in check.

"Where would the fun be in that?"

"I don't feel fun today."

"You heard, then." She walks over, wraps her arms around me, and I'm finally sure that she's there. "I am so sorry."

"You and me both." I hug her back. Tears well in my eyes, unsure whether or not they want to be shed. Do I need to let it out or do I need to start pulling myself together? Is there a point when you can tell? Surely not now, after only hours. Surely not in the brief glimmer of a lifetime.

"He was…" I don't know what to say. Nothing feels real. Not this town, not my friend, not the loss we're struggling through.

"He was an annoying prick." She takes a step back, places her hands on my shoulders. "And he was a better human being than either of us." She sighs, steps away. "I thought this would drag you back at last."

There's a bitterness in her tone that she can't quite hide and that I wish I hadn't caused, but I'm too wrapped up in Ben to deal with that now.

"You still saw him?" I ask.

"From time to time. We worked some magic together. Performance for protests, mostly, that dissident space where our interests aligned."

"Do you know what happened?"

She picks up a bag. It rattles with her regular cans of paint.

"Come with me. I will show you what I'm doing."

I follow her around the outside of the Bell. She's got that strange way of walking she always had, alternating slow and thoughtful with sudden bursts of speed. She opens the bag and rummages inside, muttering to herself. Two minutes together, and it already feels like we've always been here. That should have been how it was with me and Ben, but there's no harder chasm to cross than the one you ripped open together.

"Accounts of deaths in this town," Star says, waving a bundle of papers: printouts off the internet, clippings from old newspapers, copies of documents from before print. "I'm going to re-enact each one nine times, show the different ways it could have been. People can watch live, but I'll tape it too, keep documents, photos, recordings of the crowd's response. Death isn't just in us, it's in the people around us."

"You're saying someone else was with Ben when he died?"

"Not that I know of." She thrusts most of the papers into the bag. "Is 'More Lives Than A Cat' a good title? Too obvious, maybe?"

"I don't know. But about Ben..."

"Here." She puts her bag down at the mouth of an alley that runs between rows of houses down to the sea front, then waves a paper. "Sarah Hopper, housewife, 1922, a good place to start. You have a phone, right, even if you never call? You can record this."

"I'm not..." I frown, look at the well worn paving stones and the cobbles of the back street. "Are you going to summon her?"

"If I can, but not until act nine. That is the one I want to get right. Now come on, phone out, get filming." She coils her blue hair on the back of her head, pins it into place with a couple of pencils. "What looks more roaring twenties, shirt open or closed? Not that the twenties roared in Aldkey, but it is about evoking the era."

"Never mind the roaring twenties," I snap. "I want to talk about Ben."

"This is about Ben." She glares at me. "This is my tribute to him."

I sag. Of course this is how she grieves. When I'm feeling lost, I seek out information, try to find my way. When Star feels lost, when she feels anything that troubles her, she turns it into art. That's why our school had so much creepy graffiti: pictures of lost children, beatings, and bereavement, of mazes with no exit, of crowds from which a single figure stared, alone among many.

"I'm sorry." At least I can still say that to her.

"Yeah, well..." She kicks an empty cola can into the gutter. "I am sorry too. What did you want to ask?"

"What happened?" I whisper, scared to ask, more scared to hear the answer, to discover something dreadful.

She shrugs.

"I wish I knew. He had been going out to Multhorpe a lot, part of his campaign to stop Rackham's development. He said that he was mapping the old paths and bridleways, comparing them with what Rackham's people were building, looking for ways that they might be breaking the law. But it was not just that. I saw him sometimes when he had come back from Multhorpe, and he was drained, shaking. He was working the ghosts of that place hard, delving into the land, doing something to stop Rackham."

"It wasn't just a heart attack." I clench my fists, and I'm shaking too. "Rackham fought back, used the magic against him."

"Maybe. Or maybe he pushed himself too far. You know better than I do, Ben didn't accept limits."

Another memory I don't need the ghosts for, one so bitter I can never wash its taste away. Ben and I screaming at each other in the street, red-faced, raging.

"I can't take it anymore," I'm shouting. "We can't save the whole world at once. I don't have the energy left."

"So you're going to give up?" he snaps back. "You're choosing to let a part of it die?"

"I'm choosing to live," I reply. "Why can't you do that?"

"I'm choosing to live for others. Why can't you do that?"

But that's the past. Here and now it's me and Star, standing in a different street, and the screeching is from the gulls.

"You think it was an accident?" I ask. "That he pushed himself too hard?"

"He never shared as much with me as he did with you." She looks down the alley, towards the endless dark of the sea. "He had been quiet when I saw him lately. This battle with Rackham, it was not like campaigning against the local hunt or to change the school curriculum. It was harder, longer, grinding his will against that family's wealth. He knew he was in the right, but I do not know if he believed he could win. Maybe he pushed too far because that was easier for him than being a failure." Her head slumps and her eyes sparkle with unshed tears. "Or maybe it is the curse of the strong that they do not seek help. They push themselves until they break, until they are lost and alone, longing for a way out."

"You think..." The words are terrible, but I have to get them out. "You think he did it on purpose? That he used the magic to kill himself?"

"I do not know." She looks at me, and I feel like we're both fading into ghosts. "Dying on Hangman's Hill is so melodramatic. Most people, I would think they had chosen that, but Ben never cared about aesthetics, so..." She shrugs. "That is why the nine lives, the nine deaths. Life is uncertainty, death can be too. I want to accept that."

I shake my head. "I can't."

Chapter Three

The vicarage is set back from the road, past a wide lawn and well-tended flowerbeds. No trees hide the place from the world; that's not Cerys's style nor the style of her church, though if such churches were in style then the Church of England would be a lot better attended, and homes like this wouldn't be relics, waiting to be sold off to investment bankers and second tier footballers, like every other nice old place in the county.

I try to settle into the vicarage as I approach, to take comfort in its ghosts: a vicar from the 1860s striding home from his Sunday sermon, puffed up with the conviction that he'll soon banish the demon drink; a servant from the 1890s nervously approaching the home of her new employer, telling herself that it's alright, this one is a man of God; a Polish refugee during the Second World War, dreaming of the freedom his country will win. I should feel their emotions as my pace matches theirs, should know their lives and loves, but they remain flickering fragments. My own tension is a barrier. I'm not letting anyone in.

The porch is so familiar, from the cracks in the tiles underfoot to the smoothness of the pillar under my hand. They've cut back the ivy since I was last here and repainted the door. How long has it been? Too long. Not long enough.

I press the plastic button of the doorbell, hear the muffled ringing of the same old chime. There's a distant crash, a rush of feet, and the door bursts open. Dom, Ben's father, stares out at me, startled behind his glasses, tea towel in his hand.

"Paul!" He blinks, bobs his head.

"I'm sorry," I say. "Were you expecting someone else?"

"No, no, no, I just..." He steps back, flaps the towel. "It's good to see you. Come on in. Come on in."

I close the door behind me, follow him down the hall, past the table with the basket of household junk and the maps of places the family have travelled to, some familiar, some new to me, but old enough for the backing paper to fade and the dust to accrue. Flowers sit in a vase, bright and fresh, not yet aware that they've been severed from their stalks, that they are, to all intents and purposes, dead.

Jazz is playing in the kitchen. Not the trad jazz that Dom likes, but the experimental stuff that Ben made us all listen to. For a moment, I'm back in his bedroom, enduring Bitches Brew and arguing about Gramsci; not a ghost, just a memory, but strong enough that I can smell our spliff and the spring blossoms outside the window. I stop in the doorway, letting the tune run through me, each disjointed note hooking a beat from my heart.

"How have you been?" Dom shuffles toward the kettle, socks sliding across linoleum.

"Me?" Who cares how I feel, after what Dom's been through?

"It's been such a long time. How long, hm? You look well." He takes three mugs from the cupboard, drops a teabag into each. "Yes, you look well. What happened to the beard?"

"God, is it that long?" I haven't had a beard since Justin and I broke up, which was during that miserable year in London, nothing but urban walking, trying to drag magic through the alien scabs of brutalised streets, which means...

A glint of light grabs my attention as Dom heads for the sink. I dart forward, grab his arm, and he looks at me in surprise.

"Did you break a glass?" I ask, pointing at the glittering shards.

"Oh!" He rubs his brow, holds up the kettle, looks at it like it's an alien thing. "I was going to..."

"I've got it."

I go to the cupboard by the door, get out the dustpan and brush. Kneeling at his feet, I sweep up the shards. Some of them are large enough that I can still make out their curve, a memory of the shape they once shared.

"Sorry about that," Dom says. "I think you must have startled me."

"You weren't expecting anyone, then."

I'm surprised. People around here love Dom and Cerys, even if most don't join them at church any more. Surely they've had visitors, people bringing them meals and making them tea, watching over them like angels in their time of grief?

"It's going to sound stupid." Dom wrings his hands.

"No one's judging you." I want to hug him, but I've got a dustpan full of glass and we were never that close. Dom has always been a good person but he was my best friend's father and that creates as much distance as closeness. We related to each other through the filter of our very different angles on Ben, saw each other through the joys and frustrations he felt, kept a distance that helped keep us all sane.

"Every time the doorbell rings, some part of me thinks that it's him, that the whole thing is a mistake, that if I get to the doorstep fast enough, he'll be there."

"I get it." My words are only half true. Even once the reality of Ben's death sinks in, it won't mean to me what it does to Dom. While I understand intellectually why he feels this way, I'm still waiting for the weight of it to drop, for my world to reorient itself around loss. But I don't need to feel what he feels to make myself useful. I take a newspaper out of the recycling bin, start wrapping up the glass. "Ben lived in this house for years. If you want, I could..."

He hesitates, tempted. He can't do what I can, but he knows about it. Unlike most walkers, Ben told his family what he could do, a choice that once seemed to me like an unusual intimacy, but that I now suspect was one more way to distance himself from them. Because of that, Dom understands what I'm offering, and he's wise enough to know that magic has its price, personal magic most of all. Eventually, he shakes his head.

"I fall apart every time I see his photo. Seeing a shadow of him like that, knowing that it was going to fade and then he would be gone… It's kind of you, but no."

He stands trembling, the kettle forgotten. I take it, fill it at the sink, silently make him a cup of tea. It's all so familiar.

"Here." I lead him to a seat at the kitchen table, then press a mug into his hands. He stares through the steam, lost even to himself. There's no way he could face the questions I want to ask. "Is Cerys around?"

He looks up, blinks.

"Whatever happened with you boys?"

It's a decade since Ben and I legally became adults, and a dozen years since Dom first drove us home still drunk from a party, stifling his amusement at our groans and the stink of cheap vodka. But in his mind, we're still boys. Perhaps we always will be. Perhaps that's a kindness now, however much it annoyed Ben.

"People grow apart," I say, as if it's any kind of answer.

Dom looks out the French windows. "I wouldn't know about that."

And I understand why he's alone here right now, however tragic that is. Each generation makes the same mistakes as the one before, just faster, the details blurred.

"Cerys is out there?" I ask.

"Where else?" He shakes his head, disagreeing with something only he heard.

I squeeze his shoulder then open those windows and head out onto the patio. The garden is as orderly as ever, the path a string of stone strides across soft ground, the lawn a victory of neatly mowed grass. The hedges have recently been trimmed back, but a few wild strands break through. Off to one side, the roof above the log pile is being held up by a broom handle, even as moss bursts through its wooden tiles. A rabbit peers at me from under the hedge, twitches his nose, scurries away. Officially this isn't his home, but he'll be back.

Cerys is near the bottom of the garden, where flower beds give way to vegetables, the subsistence garden of an earlier age. She has a bucket in one hand and a trowel in the other, but weeding is an alibi. She never stoops to tend the soil, just paces around the beds looking at the results of her hard work, the space she has mastered, the living things she has raised from dead dirt. When I first met her, I mistook these slow walks around her garden for a woman comfortable in her life. Now I know that she was comforting herself.

As I approach, she doesn't stop but she does look around. She's wearing her clerical collar, seldom a good sign. Cerys likes to show the world how relaxed she is, the vicar who wears jeans and invites guitars into the church. Wearing the collar at home means she's either busy and tired, or so distracted she's forgotten to change.

"Paul. I didn't expect to see you."

On most people, a Welsh accent sounds lilting and soft. Cerys makes it stiff, formal, a voice of defiance. Like too many Englishmen before me, I'm an invader on her land.

"I came to offer my condolences."

"You think that's appropriate?"

"He was my best friend for years."

"And what happened between you broke his heart."

She turns away, but she doesn't tell me to leave, and I know from experience that she would. I follow her down the path, the two of us falling into step. This path is as old as the house, its route well worn, the magic strong. My footsteps hook into its rhythm and figures appear. I see a younger Cerys, holding the hand of a small boy, telling him what all the plants are. I see two teenagers walking the same route, reinventing those plants, giving them rude names and ruder uses. I almost smile, almost cry, but I don't dare do either around Cerys.

I'd wanted to take my time, to ease into the conversation, but there's nothing easy about her, or about me being here. If we're going to leave with hearts bleeding, then I might as well cut to the chase.

"Did Ben leave you anything, the last time he went away?" I ask, strolling along beside my teenage self. "An email, a note, a text, maybe a book he thought you should read?"

"It was a heart attack, Paul." She reaches down, rips a dandelion from the edge of a potato bed, while behind her, the ghost of young Ben plants seeds. "Heart attacks don't leave suicide notes."

"You know that these things aren't always clear cut. Mental health can put a strain on the body."

"Don't." She spins around, glares at me, and the ghosts of childhood vanish. It's just the two of us. "Don't project your issues onto him. Not again."

I look her in the eye. The me that used to walk this path would be amazed at anyone brave enough to face her.

"Ben was his own person," I say. "His issues were his own, just like everything else about him."

There's a twitch in her cheek. Cerys is a proper modern Anglican, torn by the sort of faith that's only possible through doubt. Raised amid the songs of the valley choirs, trained in an evangelical stronghold, led to serve God in the mild-mannered moderation of suburban England. Her faith is made of kindness and consideration, not fire and brimstone, but tradition pushes her heart one way, liberalism the other.

"I don't like you, Paul," she said, "but I never meant to blame you for what he became."

"There's no blame in being gay."

She frowns, turns to examine her flower beds. Her eyes sparkle like the broken glass in the kitchen. She grabs the dead head of a rose, but a thorn presses into her thumb and she jerks away.

"That's not what I meant," she snaps, lying to herself more than to me. "It's not as if you two even..." She glances at me, but now she can't hold my gaze. "Did you?"

I didn't think I'd be the one facing questions. Cerys was never interested in who her son had become, except in how it affected her. It's a bit bloody late to start caring now.

"No," I snap. "We didn't fuck."

She flinches from the word. I've become cruel in the face of her coldness, and that's not who I want to be. Somewhere in this garden, I've crossed from seeing a grieving mother to confronting the resentful elder of my youth. I need to row back, if the two of us are going to find a way forward.

"It wasn't like that," I say, more softly. "We were best friends. Anything more would have been gross."

She nods and holds her bucket out to me. "Hold this, will you?"

I do as I'm asked. She takes a set of secateurs from her back pocket and starts pruning the roses, more carefully this time.

"It wasn't just about sexuality," she says, the last word pronounced a little too clearly. "Remember that trip to France?"

"Of course."

Who could forget a holiday like that? Two weeks with my best friend, walking the pilgrim trails, surrounded by the sick and the lost, hundreds of strangers with seashells hanging from their packs. The dawning realisation that, while this walk was a holiday for us, for some it was a last, desperate burst of hope, grasping for a miracle at the end. Another realisation, as those people faded in and out of view, that not all of them wore modern clothes or physical bodies, that I had tapped into something more. And the final revelation, better than all the rest: that Ben was seeing what I did.

"I hoped that Ben would find his faith on that holiday." She snips a rose from its stalk, a flower that's just starting to wilt. "That you would both find His grace. It worked for a colleague of mine, when she had her own doubts about God's plan. But that's not what happened, is it?"

The rose crumples in her fist and she casts the petals into the bucket. I realise what I hadn't wanted to see at the time. Cerys had hoped to walk us both back to straightness, and instead she'd walked us into magic, the final piece Ben needed to find his new identity. Plenty of people have both faith and the power. Our community is full of former pilgrims who found God and magic on the same trail, but when Ben connected to the earth he found a strength that didn't need divinity to hold it up.

"No," I admit.

"I tried to save him and instead I led him astray."

"No." I shake my head. "Ben didn't go astray. He found himself."

"I always saw him as a stray soul, waiting to find his way home. I somehow hoped that I would turn around some Sunday and he would be sat in a pew. That he would meet the right girl, change his mind, and one day I'd walk my grandchildren to school."

There's so much ignorance and arrogance packed into those three sentences, I'm left shaking. It's all I can do not to fling the bucket down and storm away. But then she turns, clutching a handful of dead flowers, and there's such sorrow in her eyes that my rage melts away.

"None of that was ever true, was it?" she says.

"No." I want to tell her that I'm sorry, but the only thing I'm sorry for is that it took her this long.

"I was so busy waiting for my imaginary son, I never knew the real one." Her arms fall limp, dead petals drifting across the path. There's still something hard though, a reflection in her eyes of the bitterness in her voice. "You knew him."

I've spent so many years walking in other people's shoes, taking on their lives, their thoughts, their feelings. How high were the walls I built in my youth, that I couldn't see the truth of Cerys? She never resented me for changing Ben, something none of us could ever do; she resented me for knowing him.

Cerys hasn't always been a good person, but she was my best friend's mother, which held me as distant from her as from Dom, never quite flung apart but never close. I put the bucket down, hold out my hand, and reach across that gap.

"Let me show him to you."

She stares at my hand. What is it that holds her back? The danger of magic, a long-held resentment of me, or fear of what she might learn? So many reasons not to accept my offer. So much to lose.

Cerys takes my hand.

"Show me," she commands.

I lead her down the path, around her own garden. At first I'm tensed, expecting resistance, the two of us struggling for who will set the pace. But this is her garden, a place she's loved and nurtured for decades. She knows the heartbeat of this ground even if she doesn't know how to hear it, so I match my footsteps to hers. We fall into a rhythm and the ghosts fall into that rhythm beside us. I open my mind to them, and through the magic of our shared footsteps they flow from me to her.

Wild memories bloom between the tamed plants. Ben toddling down this path, taking his first footsteps, to the applause of his parents. Dom chasing him between the beds while Cerys laughs. The three of them walking together, talking about what vegetables to grow. Ben and I walking together, talking about love and magic, about politics and music, about what our futures hold. Ben and one of his boyfriends, caught in the last sad moments of a breakup. Ben with his grandma, showing her the flowers two weeks before she died.

Tears run down Cerys' cheeks and my heart sinks. I came to the vicarage to learn about Ben from her but she knows less than I did. There's nothing for me here.

Then I hear a fragment of conversation, echoing down the years.

"Maybe we're all pilgrims," Ben says, "religious or not. We walk to our own truths."

"Or to each other's truths," I reply, a decade ago and a footstep away.

There it is, my route to the truth, an irreligious salvation for a secular soul. If I'm going to find out why Ben died, then I'll have to walk the path that killed him.

One more vision unfolds. Not Ben this time. Dom and Cerys, back when she was pregnant, walking together, laughing. Dom reaches out, pulls a rose across the path, pricking his fingers so that she can smell the flower. I look around and there's the real Dom, the Dom of this moment, standing in the French windows, watching us with those wide, watery eyes. Cerys looks up the garden but she can't cross the gap.

I lead her towards him and her footsteps falter. The images fade around us. I squeeze her hand and she finds the rhythm again, not for me but for Ben, for the hundreds of fragments of his past preserved in this precious space. I don't stop walking when we reach the house. Instead, I reach out, take Dom's hand, walk him into memory, watch the tears stream down his cheeks. I press their hands together and step away.

As I'm creeping back through the kitchen, I glance out the window. The two of them are walking around the garden, leaning in to one another, and though grief slows their steps, the magic is stronger around them than ever before. It won't last once I'm gone, but perhaps it will leave a space in its wake, somewhere they can start to heal.

I pick up the broken glass from the kitchen counter, drop it into the bin, and walk out.

Chapter Four

If I'd known about the carnival, I never would have arranged to meet at Flinder's Field. Even first thing in the morning, with the machines motionless and the lights turned out, it's too colourful, a place of forced cheer and false faces, its every strut and sign insisting that I should scream with excitement. Its presence this week of all weeks is a cruel joke made more bitter by the memories that rise as I cross the field: the meandering merry-makers, the courting couples, the young men competing on shooting ranges and shows of strength, the children shrieking in excitement or in frustration as they're dragged home. The paper thin ghosts left by decades of carnivals, stirred up by the previous night's ambling visitors. A place of power, sure, but not a power I want any part of.

I walk faster, shaking off those images, burst through the fog of the past and stride to a stile over the far fence. Star is waiting there for me, wearing an armful of plastic bangles and sunglasses in pink frames, the sort of crap the carnival spits out as woeful rewards for winning its games. A warped vision of my own face stares back at me from the mirrored plastic lenses and the foil moon on her t-shirt.

"You know we're going for a walk, not to a rave?" I ask.

"I like to disrupt stultified expectations of the modern hiker, to cast off the waxed jackets and waterproofs, to scream to the world that we can take joy in walking." She points down. "At least I wore these."

Proper walking boots, but with luminous laces and streaks of glitter glued around the tops. Not what I would have chosen, but they'll do.

"Come on then." I climb over the stile, my footfalls reinforcing the power of the path and softening the boundary it crosses, one more moment in a struggle as old as these fields.

I come down onto lumpy ground that will be a muddy quagmire in the winter. Star pulls out coloured ribbons and starts winding them around the stile's rotting wood. "What are you doing?"

"Making art out of our odyssey," she says. "Especially the broken bits, the signs of a dying countryside, in honour of our dead friend. I might call the exhibition funeral march."

I grit my teeth. "Not everything should be fitted for a gallery space."

"My life is art, man." She waves her ribbons and the bangles on her wrist rattle. "It is important to seize every moment of inspiration."

This is why I almost hadn't invited her. I need someone who will take this journey seriously, who can help me to remember the hard realities of Ben's life and death. Sure, I could have done this on my own, followed Ben's last hike as lonely as he had been. In many ways, I would prefer to be alone with him one last time. But at the end of that hike is something that killed him. If I'm going to face it, then I want someone else whose power I can lean on, or at least someone to call an ambulance.

"Try not to slow us down," I say. "I want to reach Multhorpe by lunchtime."

"No sweat." She pulls a fistful of tissue paper from her bag, coloured strips left over from the land art project that got her in the Sunday Times; bright but ephemeral, designed to dissolve in the rain. She stops every few feet to tie them in elaborate bows on branches and hedgerows, art that will die away like the leaves with the turning seasons. When I frown, she holds them out. "Come on, help me brighten this place up! It's what Ben would have wanted."

It's not, and I suspect she knows it, that she's trying to provoke me. It's a suspicion that's confirmed when she puts the paper away, straightens her shoulders, and changes her walk, not just matching my pace so that we can walk the same memories, but imitating my every movement. She can't resist provoking people but I'm not going to let her get to me, so I press my lips tight together and keep walking.

We're not the first ones to walk this route, not by hundreds of years. The hikers' trail from Aldkey to Multhorpe follows ancient field boundaries and long-established ways, along hedgerows carefully managed since the middle ages and occasional trees that have stood sentinel for centuries. Field boundaries are the place where domestication and wilderness merge, where field mice nibble on fallen crops and hawthorn is sculpted into hedges from a sprawl of grasping branches. It's the space where people go to meet nature, and those people rise from the ground as I find my pace. I open my mind to the power of the land and it opens up the memories left here.

Most of them are unremarkable. Centuries of farm labourers heading into the fields, joyfully, wearily, resentfully, depending upon their relationships with the land, with the work, and with the people around them. Fewer from recent years, thanks to mechanisation and efficiency, intertwined trends slowly severing our last real link with the land. In place of labourers come dog walkers and hikers, just as unremarkable, just as precious. Sometimes, different ages walk in sync. The landless labourers looking for work take the same pace as map-wielding ramblers out to protect public rights of way. Perhaps it's coincidence or perhaps those ramblers tapped into something deeper than themselves, a memory of why these trails matter, how connections keep us all alive.

One Victorian walker matches his pace to that of a medieval woman, and I realise that he's doing the same as us, calling forth memories with his feet. He turns and waves, not quite looking at us but knowing that someone will be there, sometime in the future. Star laughs, waves back though he can't see her, then turns to wave at whoever will follow, long after we're gone. She blows a kiss and sprays an arc of paint through the air, performing for an audience that's at once both absent and infinite.

There are other ghosts that stand out. A couple running away from home, their hearts full of love and trepidation. Soldiers from the barracks wearing the uniforms of different eras, struggling with fear or bravado as they take one last lone walk before an overseas posting. Funny how many men who've been marching all day still come walking when the work's done.

While Star examines the crowd of ghosts, I look through them, seeking a trace of Ben. He came this way on that last day. There must be a ghost of him here.

When I find him, it's an older memory. Me and Ben, sixteen years old, carrying placards on sticks, heading for one of our first protests.

"Once they cancel the road, what next?" younger me asks, hopelessly naive. Within a year, the ancient woodland we're trying to save will be bulldozed, shortening the drive to the new supermarket.

"A fund-raising walk for animal rights," Ben says. "If people can't look after helpless animals, how can we expect them to take care of each other?"

"Cool."

"And I want to go down to London in the summer, to the Pride march."

"That would be awesome." Younger me grins. "I'm surprised you're not trying to organise Aldkey pride."

"One day." He sounds more determined than I remember. I suppose that he was always set on fixing Aldkey, while that trip to London planted the seed of my escape. It also gave me a misguided romanticism about cities which I'd only lose through urban living.

"I want to get a campaign group together against the new housing estate at Multhorpe," Ben adds.

"Why Multhorpe?" It's the first time I ask that question but it won't be the last.

"Think global, act local." It's a sound bite we've both heard before. At that age, it sounded like an answer. Listening back now, it's more of an excuse. What wasn't he telling me then? What aren't the memories showing me now?

Ben smiles and starts talking about a party the two of us had gone to the previous night, one I barely remember now. Star frowns and starts walking faster, getting ahead of me. I speed up, and the ghosts fade away.

"What's the rush?" I call out.

"You want to get to Multhorpe by lunchtime, right?" she calls back, as she strides through the shadow of a lone oak. "No time to go slow."

It's stupid. She can't maintain this pace. I speed up anyway. I'm not going to let her get ahead of me.

As I find a different rhythm, new memories appear. That's when I find the Ben I'm looking for, the Ben of a few days age, striding purposefully. There's something more real about seeing this version of him. Perhaps it's because I know how little time he has left. Perhaps he just feels closer because he's my age again. I choke back a sob, and my own emotions break my immersion in the past. Ghosts scatter, Ben evaporates, and it's just me and Star.

I clench my teeth and press my feet against the earth with greater determination, but that's not how any of this works. Intention is the enemy of openness. I'm not connecting to the world, I'm stalking through it, stamping out my frustrations.

"Come on," I snap at Star as I stride past. "We've got to match his pace, got to find him again."

"Give me a second." She's stopped to catch her breath, like I knew she would.

I keep on walking, trying to find that fragment of Ben again. I take deep breaths, try techniques I learned from a Buddhist friend, picture my frustrations as leaves on the wind and let them blow away.

There he is again, walking across the next field. I run to catch up, and sheep who were oblivious to the ghostly presence scatter to escape me. I reach out, even though I know there's nothing I can touch, because sometimes hope is a brutal friend. Sure enough, my fingers pass through his back. There's nothing. Not even a lingering softness on my skin, not a chill of fog or a tingle of smoke.

I take a deep breath, step forward into the place he occupies. I don't need to be so closely aligned, but it can help, and though it feels wrong to do it to someone I knew, I want it so badly that I don't resist. I plunge forward, occupy the space where he walked, my footsteps exactly matching his.

He's thinking about Multhorpe. About the ancient sites there and his anger at the county surveyor for neglecting them. There's power, places of importance, traces in the landscape that are going to be lost forever.

The thought is a fleeting fragment, gone almost as quickly as it arrives. There's no stillness in my mind, and the turmoil chases away my calm, chases Ben away far more easily than leaves on the breeze. There's the stabbing pain of a stitch in my side, and I stop, panting, hands on knees, drained by magic as much as my strides. The past evaporates and I'm slammed back into the present.

While I'm catching my breath Star catches up with me. She pushes those stupid sunglasses back and stands with her hands on her hips, one eyebrow raised.

"You got that out of your system?" she asks.

I keep taking long breaths. Whatever "that" is, the answer will be no. There's nothing that I want to get out.

She takes out her phone, snaps some photos of the sheep, then turns it on me.

"Don't." I hold out my hand, like some celebrity trying to fend off the paparazzi. "I'm not here for that."

"This is our tribute to Ben," she says. "It is how we honour him, how we keep his memory alive. That needs to be recorded."

"This isn't about us, it's about understanding him, knowing what he did and why." I unhook a water bottle from my backpack and take a swig. "It's serious, not one of your art projects."

"Do not dismiss my work just because you spend your time taking cheap pictures for tourist brochures."

"I'm not the one taking selfies while we try to find our dead friend."

"Maybe you should be." She waves the phone at me. "Maybe this is a memory you will want to come back to when you are far away."

"I doubt it."

"Of course. Because you want to forget this place, want to forget us, want to put it all behind you."

"Then why am I here?"

"I don't know, Paul. You tell me."

I didn't even know there was a way to take a photo angrily, but she manages it.

"I'm here for Ben," I say. "I'm here to find out why he died. Today, that's all that matters."

I hook the bottle onto my bag, turn my back on her, and start walking again. My pace is swift but steady, one I can keep up for a long time. Maybe Star can keep up with me too, maybe she can't. Right now, I don't care.

Through a gate and into the next field. We're higher up than when we started, and I glimpse the sea, past the fields and the hedgerows. The horizon is lost in the heat of the day, blue sky and blue sea merging in the distance. A gull circles overhead, watching.

"Go judge someone else," I shout at it, waving my fist. The gull catches another current in the air, glides away, and I'm left alone.

Except that I'm never alone, not when I'm walking. I settle into the movement, feet rising and falling, arms swinging by my sides, taking deep and steady breaths. There's me and the land, connecting with every step, and then there are the other people who've made that connection without ever knowing what they did. They emerge from the air and walk alongside me. A walker in Victorian skirts whistling for her dog. A farmer with a shotgun, hunting the fox that's plagued his flock. A policeman looking for clues to a theft.

And Ben, that recent Ben, walking towards Multhorpe. I don't rush to meet him this time, but keep pace just behind. I expect him to be thinking about the power of the place again, but he's staring at a piece of paper in his hand. He screws it up, hurls it into the hedge, though he always hated littering. Then he speeds up, our paces separate, and the ghost of him fades.

I could speed up to keep pace, but what good would it do? I'm learning nothing. Instead I stop, my attention caught by a glimpse of white in the hedge. I pull out the balled up paper that Ben threw away.

I unfold it reverently, this relic of my lost friend, easing out creases and straightening battered corners. It's a letter, on the headed paper of a legal firm. It's threatening legal action against Ben if he doesn't stop interfering in the business of Steven Rackham and Rackham Enterprises. There are allegations of trespass, criminal damage, industrial espionage. There's talk about specific courts and compensation that I know Ben could never afford, any more than he could afford lawyers' fees. Landowners like Rackham wield their own sort of magic, using barriers and borders to hack the land apart, to sever the strands walkers weave, but they also wield more material power. Why fight with ghosts when you can field lawyers and bankers instead?

Maybe this isn't just about the land, maybe it's about who shapes it. At Multhorpe, that's the Rackhams. They shaped the land when they were gentry snatching up fields through acts of enclosure. They're reshaping it again now that rented farmland is less profitable than housing estates, retail parks, and road building.

I start walking again, more slowly, rereading the letter as I go. According to Rackham's allegations, Ben had been out to Multhorpe a lot lately. That's not a surprise in itself, but the extent of it, written out like this, reads like an obsession. Ben had people all over the country asking for his help, so of all the causes he could choose, why was this his final fight?

Footsteps reach me from behind: not a ghost, but Star, her t-shirt sticking to her skin, hands in her pockets.

"What you got there?" she asks.

"Letter from Rackham's solicitor, telling Ben to back off."

"Lawyers. Pack of assholes, the lot of them."

Our footsteps sync as we cross a gently sloping hill and a building site comes into view. I can't hear her inner voice, like I might if I was matching pace with a ghost. Still, there's something to the rhythm of our steps, a connection that's not about land or magic or memory, but about sharing the experience of being in a body, of moving through the world.

"I'm sorry," I say. "Your art is important."

"Damn right it is."

"I wish I'd been here to see more of it."

"No you don't." She pulls a paint can out of her bag, only to put it away again. "I am sorry too. I know this is something bigger, deep magic and grief. I think maybe I am jealous."

"Jealous?" I glance at her, then away, but there are no ghosts to clear up my confusion.

"I stayed here the whole time. I saw how things went down. I started making plans to remember him. But then you came back, and suddenly it was all about you."

"Star, I--"

"Shut up and listen. I know, in here..." She taps her chest. "I know that you two were closer, back then, and I tried not to be jealous. You were my friends, when no one else was, and I will always be grateful for that. But I stood on the edge of a magic circle, some crystal realm the two of you lived in. It was beautiful. I was jealous while it lasted, and then furious when you broke it, because it was always about you.

"This way of things makes sense. You come from here. You truly belong. When you come back, the world reshapes to embrace you. But me, I can never go back where I came from, so I guess I am jealous of that too."

We've almost reached the building site, but we stop walking. After this, there won't just be ghosts, there will be people, and we need time to ourselves still.

"I'm sorry," I murmur, arms hanging by my sides. "I had no idea."

"Me neither. But that is the magic of walking, isn't it? You find yourself. Problem is, we were trying to find Ben." She pulls her sunglasses back across her eyes. "What now, oh mighty leader?"

I hunch, look back the way we came.

"I don't know," I confess. "I was convinced that walking to Multhorpe would tell us why Ben was so obsessed with the place, and that would tell us what to do next. But we're at the end of the road, and that hope has gone walkabout."

"Maybe..." Star grins. "But the end of the road is the start of the road too, right?"

She walks back the way we came, and I follow her, hesitantly. I don't want to walk all the way back yet. This is where Ben died. I'm sure it's where I need to be. But I can't keep holding Star at the edge of our magic circle. I have to trust her.

I let my thoughts go, find my rhythm, and straight away, a ghost appears. It's Ben, ten or eleven years old, around the age we met. He's walking away from Multhorpe and he keeps glancing back. He looks scared. He picks up speed. I match him, and so does Star, the two of us running alongside the frightened boy. I wish with all my heart that there was something I could do to help him, but the past can't be changed. Our only negotiation with it is one of acceptance.

I look back. Other people are running after Ben, keeping a distance though they could easily catch up with him. Three lads in their late teens, dressed in branded jeans and t-shirts, shouting and laughing. It's a barbed and vicious laughter. One of them throws a stone at Ben, then another. This one catches him on the forehead and blood runs across his eye, down his cheek. It's awful to watch. These three are so much bigger, so much stronger, and they should know so much better. I can't imagine how terrifying this must be for Ben, and I can't imagine what it takes to act like this.

But I know what sort of person does it, because I recognise one of those faces. Younger then, but with the same arrogant twinkle in his eye, Steven Rackham throws another stone and laughs.

Chapter Five

I've seen ugliness before, seen the pain and fear of the past. We all have. Run down the wrong street and you'll find yourself running with a battered woman fleeing her husband. Walk across a battlefield or the site of an old hospital and you'll be swallowed by flashes of pain. You learn the art of the sudden stop, of walking out of sync, of avoiding certain places and their past. There are things I've seen, if only for a second, that were more brutal than this. But they weren't personal. They weren't someone I love.

"Did you know?" Star asks, as we head across the field, feet dragging in the dirt.

How can I even answer? Of course I knew that Ben was bullied, that he was an outsider. All three of us were. That was why we were friends. Star knows better than to ask something so obvious, but surely she should also know better than to ask about a specific incident. There are too many moments we didn't talk about, even to each other, even when we were all there. The ones without witnesses, you don't share, because sharing makes them more real, and that gives them power. We could be happy so long as we respected those silences.

Couldn't we?

"It must have been before I knew him," I say, and touch my forehead, in the same place where the rock hit Ben. "He already had that scar through his eyebrow when we met."

"I wonder what he told his parents."

"Probably told them it was an accident." I recall Cerys telling a story along those lines once and Ben looking away. I'd thought he was embarrassed by a moment of clumsiness. "You know Cerys. She never meant to make him feel like crap..."

"But she always saw why he was at fault."

"Yep."

"Parents, man. They fuck you up."

I'm not going to disagree. I remember the blazing rows I'd hear while waiting outside Star's front door, words I couldn't understand but whose tone was as clear as day.

"So I'm told." I shrug.

"How is your mom?"

I shrug at that too. "Quiet. Same as she's been since dad, you know..."

I wanted to walk with him too, after the cancer, but the ghosts of hospital corridors were too much. I didn't dare try the hospice.

At least with dad, I'd known what was coming. I found jobs close to the town my parents had moved to, stayed in their spare room while I wrote. I'd had a chance to spend time with him, to say goodbye, and in spite of it all, I'd felt helpless.

"We'll find him again," I say as we walk past the construction site. "Ben, I mean."

"We will." Star looks at the torn ground, the straight-edged holes, the piles of bricks. "Shouldn't somebody be working here?"

"Maybe they've gone for lunch."

"Where? This is Multhorpe. It has one corner shop and a pub that only opens at four."

"Sounds like you're the one with the answers, not me."

We keep walking. This used to be a meadow, with a playground for kids at the end. People came here to walk their dogs. Now it's mud and weeds and tire tracks, half-built foundations and heaps of abandoned bricks.

At the end of the field is the road and a few more houses. This part of Multhorpe isn't the sort of straw-roofed, village green place I'd photograph for a tourist brochure. It's a loose scatter of cottages along narrow, winding roads, isolated places built for the servants and labourers who once worked the Rackham estate. Nice enough buildings, in an old stone and loose slates sort of way. One of the places we pass is clearly abandoned, the roof sagging, one window smashed, the garden overgrown. The next one has a large, grubby white van outside, and a couple piling possessions into the back.

"Excuse me," I say, and they look at me like I've landed from an alien planet, or maybe that look is for Star.

"Yeah?" the woman asks.

"Do you know anything about protests against the new developments?"

"Nothing to do with us." The woman turns back to lifting a rug into the van.

"You never met a guy called--"

"All we want is to get something for my family's house," the woman says tersely. "Is that too much to ask?"

"You've sold it to the developers?"

She sighs and turns, arms folded, while her partner drags the rug down the van, his steps awkward and irregular.

"I want to get paid," she says. "And if I get involved with that nonsense, then even the shitty deal we got is off. So I'm telling you what I told your obnoxious friend: piss off and leave us alone."

"Aren't you a delight?" Star says. "Do you kick puppies in your spare time?"

The woman glares at her, eyes narrowed.

"It's OK," I say. "I'm sorry. We'll go."

I get it. Life can't have been great out here, but at least it had a certain sense of peace. Now that's being trashed. Getting out while you can is a reasonable response, but Ben never saw "reasonable" as the right response to power, and I bet he pushed these people hard.

Star and I walk on. When I glance back over my shoulder, the woman is closing the door of the van. I see ghosts too, a couple in ragged clothes walking away from the house, her carrying a squirming bundle of life, him carrying a sack that's too light to contain a family's whole existence. Behind them are a band of toughs with tricorn hats and hefty sticks. The methods change but the dynamics stay the same.

The drainage ditch between the road and the hedge is full of disintegrating leaves and something else that's died among them. Flies buzz and I hold my nose as I pass, trying not to gag. I wonder what it was: a pet, a stray farm animal, maybe a fox that got hit by a car. The thought niggles at me, distracts me, and I don't realise where I am until we're around the corner and approaching the junction by the King's Head.

I brace myself, knowing that there's one memory I couldn't avoid out here. While part of me wants to turn away, there's another part that can't resist picking at the scab. It already hurts like hell, so why not wrench it open and let it bleed?

I slow down. Star looks at me uncertainly, then she slows too. We find the rhythm of the road, of the land beneath, of the memories flowing through this place. Of hikers and drifters, farmhands and seasonal labourers. Of people stopping for a drink after a long afternoon's work or walk.

Sure enough, out of the shifting crowds of centuries, three figures emerge from the doorway of the pub. Me, Ben, and Star, all with pint glasses in our hands. This one's from six years ago. I could tell you the exact date, it's that firmly stamped in my mind.

This is Ben just as his fame is kicking in, England's youngest county councillor and a leader in the national anti-oil movement, the walking embodiment of "think global, act local". That summer, he's spoken at two party political conferences, and a Guardian profile piece is in the works. He's handsome, passionate, dedicated, every young idealist's dream, and I want to celebrate what he's done, but I feel like I'm losing a part of myself. Without the words to express that, I've found another way to cope.

"I can't believe you're doing this," Ben says. "I can't believe you're abandoning it all, you... you... you traitor!"

"Oh, yeah, why would I want to leave when I could stick around and put up with shit like that!"

Younger me waves his pint glass, beer sloshing over the side. We're on our third drink, and though that's not why this is happening, it'll be a good excuse later, when I'm looking for a way to calm myself down.

"Guys, guys, chill!" Younger Star gets between us, hands raised, stumbles as she tries to keep up while walking backwards. Ben and I pick up speed, stalking angrily down the street. "You are going around in circles."

"At least I'm going somewhere," younger me says. "I'm going to London, I'm going to live with Justin, and I'm going to find something better than this miserable, backwater town."

"Fuck London and fuck Justin!" Ben declares.

"Oh, you'd like that, wouldn't you!"

"Yeah, right, like I'd go for a stuck up, coffee shop poser like him."

"At least I can form a relationship."

"Because you're too busy thinking with your cock to think about what matters in the world."

"Guys, please!" Younger Star clutches her hands together. Older Star watches her as we stalk the trio down the lane. Her eyes are hidden behind her sunglasses, but there are wrinkles in her brow.

"What matters in the world?" younger me shouts. "It's more than just politics, you self-righteous prick."

"Great excuse. Is that how you forgive yourself for giving up?"

"I'm not giving up! I'm finding some balance before I go completely insane." Younger me taps the side of his head, and I'm so caught up in the memory that I mimic the gesture. I can feel the rawness in his throat, in his chest, in his heart. "We never get to win, and it's destroying me. I need something else in my life. And you need something else in your life, before you burn yourself out."

126

"Don't you dare tell me what I need, not when you're fucking off to London for a guy with more beard than brain cells."

"You might be happy stuck in your rut forever." Younger me's voice goes cold and hard. He thinks he's found something precious, something to last him a lifetime, and now it's under attack. "But I'm leaving."

We've reached a fork in the road. One ghost stomps away to the left, the other to the right. Younger Star sinks onto the verge, head in her hands. Older Star touches the air where her ghost's shoulder is before the echoes of our footsteps fade and the memory disappears.

I wrap my arm around Star's shoulder.

"I'm sorry you had to see that," I say. "Twice."

"Twice?" She laughs. It's a hollow sound. "You think I have not walked this memory since?"

"I couldn't."

"I get that." She puts her arm around me and leans her head against my shoulder. "You were not the last one to fall out with him, just the most dramatic. It is why I did not see him much anymore. I stepped back before the fireworks went off."

"So he was alone?"

She takes off her glasses and rubs fiercely at her eyes, like she can drive the tears back in. "Pretty much."

"Fuck."

I sit on the verge where she sat six years before. My arms hang limp between my legs, knuckles pressing on the rough surface of the road. I feel hollow, like all the life has been sucked out of me. Across the road, insects crawl across the stump of a dead tree.

"Maybe if I'd stuck around," I say. "If I'd been more patient, he wouldn't have been alone."

"It is not your fault. Once Ben found a cause, he had to throw his whole heart into it, and there were always more causes to find. People admire that kind of obsession, but few can live with it."

"If we'd talked about it more, back then, if I'd explained better what was bothering me..."

"He would not have heard you." She squats in the road and takes my hand. "Listen to me. He was always going to grind himself into the ground. It is good that you did not let him drag you down."

"Maybe." I'm not convinced, but I'm not going to throw another friendship away on an argument no one can win. "Come on, let's keep walking."

We get up and head down the lane. Star keeps glancing at me, failing to hide her worries. I force a smile.

"Seriously, it's fine."

It won't be fine. I abandoned Ben, because I couldn't stand my own guilt at needing more than a righteous cause, couldn't face the way my tarnished image looked in the mirror of his righteousness. And maybe because he was jealous of what I had, the things he was too scared to let into his life. But how can you say things like that to someone you care about? How can you even see them when they're the very light you view the world by? And how can you fix a friendship when the feelings connecting you sharpen every crossed word to a razor edge?

I was a coward, and as ashamed as I was scared. Instead of talking, I left Ben to sink into isolation and obsession. If that's why he died, if he couldn't take it any more and he had to find a way out, then that's on me.

I have to know the truth.

We're heading towards Morley's Farm. It's a sort of secular pilgrimage site, a place where local socialists and anarchists gather every May Day to remember their past, and where the walkers of ways join them to tap into the power of their march. Back in the 1830s, labourers on the Rackham estate formed a sort of union, to stand up for their rights and their wages. The Rackham of that era found out and it went as well as those things ever do: two people crippled, one dead, four deported to Australia by a judge was also happened to be a Rackham, then back to business as usual, with usual meaning long hours and grinding poverty. Morley was the man who died, and his farm's stood like a gravestone for nearly two hundred years, a monument to courage and comradeship, or perhaps to desperation.

We round the corner, past a tangled copse, and stare slack-jawed at a wide gash of earth tearing through the fields, at the rubble where the farm used to be. Yellow diggers with big black wheels stand silent as the dead, their blades stained brown with the blood of the land.

"What the..." I look around, trying to make sense of the impossible. This is Morley's Farm. It's a piece of history. I was going to put it in my guide book.

The place doesn't feel right. My stomach's heavy, my skin tingling. I can't tell if that comes from seeing my past smashed up to build a road or if there's something wrong with the magic.

"They can't do this," I say.

"Course they can." It's an unfamiliar voice. I look around, see a man in a hard hat and a hi vis vest sitting on one of the diggers, drinking coffee from a plastic cup. "Gotta build the road, ain't you?"

"This can't be legal."

"You sound like that shouty wanker with the petition. I'll tell you what I told him: as long as I'm getting paid, I don't care."

It's the sort of ignorant, short-sighted logic that drove Ben to despair, that led to lectures about moral responsibility and how societies descend into dictatorship.

"This guy with the petition, did he compare you to the Nazis?" I ask.

"You've met him?" Hi vis shakes his head. "What a wanker." He turns his head. "Hey, love, get off there. It's not safe wandering around a building site."

"You know what is not safe? Calling me love." Star sticks her middle finger up at the guy, who returns the gesture with a smile. With her other hand she beckons me onto the broken earth. "Paul, you have to see this."

I follow her lead, boots sinking into loose dirt, and instantly I'm overwhelmed. There are ghosts everywhere, figments of the past striding this way and that. Two hundred years of May Day marchers and their magical hangers on, jumbled chaotically together. Some walk half in the soil and half out, others up and down the air. Some are only fragments of people, bodies jumbled together. Their chants have also been broken into discordant fragments, like a sound file of crowd noise remixed by an avant garde DJ. Ghosts flicker in and out of existence and snatches of that sound come and go with them.

"You ruined it." I stare at the guy in the high vis vest. "You tore up the land and all its memories."

"Whatever." He shakes his head and pours himself another coffee from a thermos flask. "Can you believe there's not even a Greggs out here? We're fixing that. You should say thank you."

"You unbelievable--"

"Paul," Star snaps. "Pay attention."

"To what? It's sheer chaos!"

"Exactly. Think it through."

It's hard to think about anything amid these broken visions, the crowds of the past coming at me from every angle. I've never seen anything like it.

And that's what Star means. We've both been to road protests before, trespassed on building sites, walked through ruins. This isn't how they work. When the land becomes broken, the memories fade, the ghosts are lost forever. It would take incredible power and determination to keep them here, when the very land they walked has been ripped apart.

This is Ben's work. It has to be.

I smile. I feel like he's here with us, more than I did while seeing his ghost.

Then the other shoe drops.

"Where are your colleagues?" I ask.

Hi vis guy shakes his head.

"Big meeting with management. Nobody wants to work here. They say that the place is haunted. People keep having accidents."

Of course they do, because Ben's made the ghosts here so powerful that I can see them without walking. Half the work crew will have been having visions, getting distracted while they're operating diggers and drills.

"Wankers," hi vis guy growls. It's clearly his favourite word.

"You've not seen anything?" I ask.

"No," he says, more firmly than he needs to. He won't look at me.

Star takes out a thick, battered pad and a pencil, then starts sketching what she sees, recording this for posterity. There's no saving Morley's Farm, but the people who used to come here will want to know what happened. Maybe it could spark a new protest, get this road reconsidered. Ben kept the memories alive here, and maybe those memories can keep hope alive for the old Multhorpe, whatever's left of it.

Star's face crumples in frustration. She was never one for traditional art forms and the sketches are going slow. She shoves the pad into her pack, pulls out her phone and starts taking photos instead.

"Here, what are you doing?" hi vis guy calls out.

"What does it look like?"

"You can't take photos here. It's private property."

"That is not a thing."

"I'm making it a thing." He starts climbing down off the digger.

"And I am making images for our friend's funeral."

"Funeral?" That catches him off guard.

"Our friend with the petition," I say. "He died."

"Oh. Shit. Sorry." Hi vis guy takes off his hard hat. "I didn't mean what I said, about him being a wanker."

I shrug, thinking back to our argument down the road and half a lifetime ago.

"We all have bad days."

"Still, I..." Hi vis scratches his head. "Does the parish lady know?"

"Parish lady?" I'm far too distracted by the ghosts to guess at what he means.

"Two people have made this job a pain, your mate with the petition and the lady from the parish council. I never saw it, but they must have been working together."

"Do you know her name?"

"Theresa something. Grey hair, big boots, one of them green jackets posh blokes wear. She's usually out around the village somewhere, being a pain."

"I guess we'd better talk to her then." I walk across the rest of the construction site, to the far side of this gaping wound. Star follows me, then stops as we emerge from the cloud of jumbled ghosts. She turns and waves at our informant.

"Thank you for your help," she says. "Hi vis wanker."

Chapter Six

If Multhorpe has a heart, then it's the part after Morley's Farm. The houses here huddle together like they're sharing a secret or perhaps seeking shelter from a worrying world. Weathered stones anchor thatched roofs amid low-walled gardens that hold as many vegetable patches as flower beds. Trellises bloom with nasturtiums, clematis and roses, blossoms arching over gates and trailing across walls.

Once upon a time, this place represented progress. Entrepreneurs enclosed the land in the name of efficiency and economy, but they cared about aesthetics too. A cluster of quaint cottages looked lovely from the back of a carriage, and helped to contain one's workers without tarnishing the view. If one happened to squeeze rent from them, that was only fair, particularly considering the effort and expense taken to knock down the old village and build this new one in its place.

"How are we going to find this Theresa woman?" Star asks.

"Give me a moment."

I can't resist taking my camera from my pack and snapping a few photos. This is the English village that tourist guides are made of, quaint and quiet, lush with life and layered with history, an oil painter's dream. Ben used to argue that those images were a lie, because they only represented half the story, but what story ever tells you everything? These chocolate box cottages with their floral gardens are the reality of Multhorpe just as much as the broken houses we saw before Morley's Farm. It's important to see the world through both lenses.

I walk slowly, observing each house in turn, pausing to frame shots through the branches of trees or the gaps between fences. I pause, crouch, take a photo through a gateway, another up close on a moss-flecked cherub on a garden wall. When I lower the camera, I find a ghostly figure sharing my slow, broken pace. It's Ben, pausing to make a note of something he's seen, perhaps about the ghosts of this place. Then he speeds up and vanishes from view. Instinctively, I move to match his pace, then stop myself. Being drawn into his wake took me to a dark place before and in the end it broke our friendship. I need to be careful, both for his sake and for mine.

A spray can rattles as Star shakes up the paint. She's grinning as she contemplates the possibilities a long stretch of fence provides. Then she glances up, eye caught by the same movement I've just seen.

"Is that her?" Star asks.

A woman is emerging through the trellised arch at the entrance to one of the gardens, closing the low wooden gate behind her. She fits the description: big boots, the sort I associate with horse riders; green waxed jacket, though it's hardly needed in this weather; yellow scarf; grey hair, tied neatly back. The fact that she's clutching a fistful of leaflets reinforces the impression that we've found the right woman.

I walk over. I've spent so much of the day deep in magic, I don't even have to try to summon the ghosts. They swirl around me with every step, Multhorpe's inhabitants down the centuries. Women carrying baskets that could be for harvests or for laundry. Men with spades and scythes over their shoulders. Children waving sticks and chanting rhymes. Between them, glimpsed through the gaps of other people's lives, fractured flashes of Ben. I don't want to break away, to dismiss them, to let him go, but they're a distraction, and I have to make an effort to concentrate as I approach the woman.

"Excuse me," I say. "We're looking for someone called Theresa who's been campaigning against the new development."

"You are, are you?" She walks through another gate, up a garden path, and pushes a leaflet through a letter box. As she walks back down the path, she runs her gaze down me, assessing, evaluating, then does the same to Star, who's still clutching a paint can. "You don't look like the sort Rackham would hire; he prefers a banal style of thug."

Star gives her spray can one last defiant shake, then shoves it into her bag. She's willing to compromise just as long as she can still show her resentment.

"We're nothing to do with Rackham," I say.

"Good." The woman heads up the next garden path, drawing another leaflet from her pile.

"We're friends of Ben Hudson."

"Of course you are." A letter box snaps shut. She walks back towards me, past me, on to the next house.

"Are you Theresa, then?"

"I am."

"Could we ask you some questions about what's been happening around here?"

"I'm busy." The snap of another letterbox. Brisk strides as she makes her way past.

"We could help." It's just a few leaflets, a good way to win her around, and she'll have to talk to us if we're working together.

She stops, scowls, lips pressed tight together. Then she reaches into her canvas satchel with its frayed edges and pulls out a bundle of leaflets. She hands half to Star and half to me. They're advertising a public meeting at the King's Head, about the new development.

"Very well," she says. "You two can deliver down the other side of the road. Be careful putting them through the letterboxes, no none likes to read a scrunched up mess. When you've done that side, you can work your way along Ash Crescent and Maple Drive."

She turns away, heads up the next path, and I see the problem with my offer. I'd hoped to talk with her while we deliver the leaflets, but this isn't an activity that allows for much conversation. Too late now. I made an offer and I need her good will, so Star and I head across the street.

At first, the two of us try to alternate houses, but that turns out to be more confusing than it should be, so instead, Star strides off to the opposite end of the road and we work our way toward each other. I quickly find out why Theresa told us to take care: getting a flimsy piece of paper through a stiff letterbox and the brush behind it is difficult, doubly so if I don't want it to get screwed up. I nearly get my fingers trapped several times, and I jerk back in alarm when a dog barks in protective fury from behind a door. So much for an easy task. My resentment rises when we finish this road and discover that the other two we've been assigned are across the village, but we do what we've been asked. As we're heading down Ash Crescent, finally into the rhythm of the deliveries, I see ghosts of those who've done the same: postmen, political campaigners, a paper boy from the 1970s with a satchel full of local news. I catch a ghostly glimpse of Ben, and for a moment it seems like he's smiling. Aren't we what he wanted, more people trying to change the world?

When we're done, we head back to the start. Theresa's outside the village shop, pacing slowly back and forth, her gaze drifting along the street. It takes me a moment to realise that she's watching the ghosts of a family walk by, dressed in Victorian Sunday best. If she sees them, then maybe she knew what Ben was, what he was capable of.

"You have magic too," I say, and I don't know why I sound so surprised.

She scowls again. "Why wouldn't I?"

"Because almost no one..."

My words trail off. I've always liked to think that this power made me special, a hangover from teenage arrogance and insecurity. But Ben, Star and I all found each other in the same small town, is it so strange to discover someone else down the coast? Perhaps this stretch of land calls out to those who can hear it, or perhaps we're not as special as we thought.

"Come with me." Theresa starts walking. I glance at Star, who shrugs, and we follow. I expect Theresa to hand us each another bundle of leaflets, ready for the next road, but instead she points ahead.

"You see that chap?"

Watching ghosts half my life has taught me a lot about the clothes of past eras. This guy's breeches and coat put him somewhere around the middle of the eighteenth century, and the state of them shows that he's not wealthy. He's carrying a brace of rabbits, snares hanging around their necks, and a single pheasant. I can't see his face as we follow him down the road, but I hear whistling, the last echo of notes drifting down the centuries, fragments floating on the breeze.

He stops, turns, looks through us. He's saying something, but the words are lost. He drops his catches, raises his hands. His head jerks back and he buckles over as he's hit, repeatedly, by someone we can't see. He falls in the dirt and curls up, clutching his head, continues to jerk and spasm beneath blows as he fades from view.

I don't need to see who struck him. I know this dynamic well enough to know that they outnumbered him and that they were sent by some figure of authority.

"That's how it's always been," Theresa says. "A battle for control of the land. Whether it's poachers against gamekeepers or cottage dwellers against developers, it's always people who live here against those meddling from the outside, the ones who want to control our land."

When she says "our land" she doesn't mean the people who own it. They're outsiders as much as anyone else. It's the people who live here. Ownership is mere accounting; what makes a place yours is inhabiting it.

"You're facing a difficult battle now, against Rackham?" I ask.

She looks at me like I'm an idiot, and I'm not sure she's wrong. This situation looks straightforward, but there's clearly something about it I'm missing.

"My family have lived in this village for hundreds of years," she says. "So have most of my neighbours."

"So have the Rackhams."

She snorts. "They don't live in this place, they leech off it. They built a mansion of foreign stone, filled it with servants from the big city, decorated it with art of all the other places and people they possess, but they've never cared for what matters. They want a piece of land, an accountant's abstraction, not a community."

"But you and your neighbours..."

"The land makes us who we are, and we make it what it is. We hold each other's memories, growing with every step we take."

"And now Rackham wants to wipe that away," I say, recognising an all too familiar story. "To tear the village down or to disrupt it so badly that you lose your connection."

"Deliberate amnesia. Wiping away our past to make room for his future."

I've been to places like that, where no ghosts walk the paths and no memories haunt the homes. Zombie villages, empty husks of what life could be.

"Ben was helping you fight back."

She snorts. "Oh, he wanted to save our past, but he wanted to do it by freezing us in time, by ensuring that nothing here ever changed again. But memory isn't just the past, it's a trail we lay into the future. We have to keep changing, building on what came before. Only an imbecile would try to keep this place as it is right now, a pretty village with no jobs and no prospects, no reason for the children to stay. We need progress that meets our needs, instead of inflicting someone else's business opportunity on us."

"So, you and Ben weren't working together?"

"The way he talked about it, you'd think that we were. Spouting fine statements about support and allyship and helping us fulfil our needs. Once he realised that I had the walking power, he was constantly pushing that plan of his, talking about how the power of the community could help him stop Rackham. But he didn't listen."

I wish it wasn't so convincing, but when Ben got an idea into his head, it could be hard to make him let go. Maybe that's a universal of humanity, but he was the person I cared about most, and that made him the one I tried hardest to convince when we disagreed. Maybe it was like the song said, maybe love tore us part, or maybe it was stubbornness. Maybe those two things aren't so very different.

An engine's roar hurtles towards us down the winding country lane. It's too narrow for cars to pass each other, never mind see what's coming, but there's a certain lunatic confidence that possesses native drivers. The three of us lurch back and a battered old Honda shoots past, dirt and leaves whirling behind it. I'm pressed against a low wall, and against the roots of a nearby tree, which are probing for weaknesses amid the weather-worn bricks.

Theresa leads us back towards the houses. She's made her point with the ghost of the poacher and there's nothing any of us can do for him. He's been dead for hundreds of years, whether he survived that beating or not.

"What was Ben's plan?" I ask.

"A grand act of magic." Theresa shakes her head. I've never met anyone with the power who was so dismissive of it. "Walking deep into history to reinforce the past. Power running from a central point, out across the whole of the Rackham estate and beyond. Reviving memories, reinforcing the landscape, linking it all together. Something that would reconnect the land, that would make the work of changing this place harder and the people more resistant. Your friend thought that it would protect us, would stop Rackham doing what he wants."

"Wouldn't that be a good thing?"

"We wanted to negotiate with Rackham, to force him into a development plan that actually suits the people who live here."

"Being protected would give you a stronger hand in negotiations."

She stops walking, sighs, turns to face me and Star. There's a weariness in her eyes.

"This isn't just about us, it's about the Rackhams and their connection to the land. Steven Rackham is a stubborn man. Defying him might have given us strength, or it might have made things a hundred times harder."

"You don't seem like a woman who backs down from a fight."

She narrows her eyes and for a moment I think she's about to prove me right. Then she looks away, to the clumps of grass and dandelions breaking through curbstones at the side of the street.

"Some fights are more dangerous than others." She speaks softly as she touches a hand to her neck, underneath the yellow scarf, revealing the brief hint of scars. "That wasn't a fight we wanted. It wasn't a magic I wanted." She looks up and her tone is sharp again. "So of course your friend ignored us, and he went out to Hangman's Hill, where he tried to bind the power."

I don't want to ask but I have to. It's a pattern I'm becoming painfully familiar with.

"Is that how he died?" My own words come out flat. If I let the emotion show, then it will overwhelm me. On some level, Theresa must understand, because her voice softens again.

"It is. I'm sorry. He went there to dig into a deeper magic, too powerful for one person to bear. He threw his magic against Rackham's and in the end it killed him."

It's the closest I've come so far to understanding, but that's not the only reason why it's comforting. Ben died for a cause he believed in. It's too soon, too young, and it will take me a long time to accept what it means, but, ultimately, it's the right ending for him, and one day I'll be able to live with that.

"He died to protect this place," I whisper. "To protect the people here."

We're at the end of a row of houses where the core of Multhorpe fades into countryside. There are beautiful old homes to one side of me, a field of spring vegetables to the other, a patch of woodland to my back. Beneath my feet is a road that's been used for centuries, whose ghosts hover at the edge of perception, waiting to be awakened by the rhythm of my feet. A remnant of the England we all dream of, concreted over by developers, replaced by the plastic dreams of Greggs and Starbucks. Ben fought to change the world, to make it more accepting, but he fought to preserve it as well. I think he'd be happy to know that's how he died. Even his parents could find comfort in that.

"Nonsense," Theresa snaps. "Nobody here asked him to risk his life for this. Nobody here wanted it."

"Then what did he die for?" I snap back. "To impress you?"

"He died for himself." Her arms are folded and she's glaring at me. "That boy had been looking for a way out of this cold, hard world since the day he was born. We were just an excuse for him to walk out of the door."

"You don't know that. You didn't know him."

"I've lived as long as you two put together. I've seen how people respond to the world. I've seen that ghastly mix of shame and certainty, the voice that tells someone they have to be perfect, but also that they'll never be good enough. I've walked these trails every day with the ghosts of my community. I've heard their thoughts, I've felt the weight in their hearts, I've lived among them until they were part of me. I know that voice, young man, the one that drives people to greatness, to oblivion, or to both."

"You don't know Ben!" I'm shouting now, just like I shouted at him. I can't help myself. It's all too raw. My heart is screaming and this is the only way to let it out. "You don't know why he did it."

"He walked these trails too, walked them over and again, learning the land for his magic. Do you really think that he didn't leave ghosts of his own?" Theresa presses two fingers against the side of her head. "Do you think I don't know what was happening in here?"

I look to Star for backup, but she's pulled away from us, arms folded tight across her chest, shoulders hunched and face still. With her eyes hidden behind her sunglasses, I can't tell if she's looking at me.

Theresa's wrong. I was wrong to even consider it. Ben wouldn't do this on purpose. He wouldn't pick this path to kill himself. But when I hunt through my memory for some way to prove her wrong, I can't find it. The memories I need are out of reach.

I start pacing, trying to stir something from within, and instead stir something outside of me. A ghost of Ben, walking down that road, head down, caught in his own obsession. I could join my footsteps with his, tap into his thoughts and feelings to prove Theresa wrong.

Couldn't I?

I stop dead, and Ben keeps walking, rubbing at his scarred eyebrow. I'm relieved when his ghost fades from view.

"Are you saying..." Star takes a deep breath. "Are you saying that he..."

"Suicide or self-destruction, it all looks the same where magic's involved." Theresa spreads her hands wide.

"You're still wrong." The words crawl like beetles out of my throat, hard-shelled and determined. "He tried to save your village but the magic killed him. You don't want to admit that because it means you could be doing a lot more than leafleting. It means you're a scared, weak old lady, and he proved how pathetic you are."

I fling one of her leaflets in her face. She stares at me, granite-faced.

"I really am sorry for your friend." Her voice is flat as a frozen river. "But don't you ever dare speak to me like that again."

She spins on her heel and strides away.

I stand in the middle of the road, feeling like someone's grabbed my guts and given them a vicious twist. The wind blows blossom from a tree, petals falling like tears.

Theresa's wrong. She has to be. Ben didn't want to die. He had too many damn fights still to win, and when we get to the heart of this, we'll see that for sure.

"Come on, Star. We have to go on, to Hangman's Hill."

Chapter Seven

Hangman's Hill glares down across Multhorpe from the east, an angular protrusion from the otherwise rolling terrain, something jagged and misplaced.

"Ben and I talked about doing a performance piece here," Star says. "A fund raiser for an international campaign against capital punishment. Remind people of all the injustices that took place in this country."

"What stopped you?" I ask.

"He was busy, I was busy, other things got in the way." She walks a few more steps, in the odd pace of alternate slowing and hurrying that signals her distraction. "I guess, in the end, it was an attempt to recapture past glories, and they did not feel all that glorious any more."

Every response I think of is even more maudlin, dragging up regrets that Ben and I never found our glory again, and jealousy that Star still had a relationship with him. I raise my camera, as much to hide my face as to take a photo of the hill, and as I zoom in, I see a ghostly figure on the trail ahead of us: Ben striding determinedly towards his death. I feel sick as I press the button and the camera clicks, knowing that he won't show up in the photo. Half a mile ahead of me and yet too far away to ever reach.

Star and I fall into step side by side as the ground starts to rise. That gives me the energy to lift one foot after the other, to head off the narrow road and onto the dirt footpath, little more than a line worn through the grass of the fields.

Star slows down and I turn to look back. She's got a hand pressed against her side. Her chest is rising and falling hard.

"Sorry," she says, in the gap between breaths. "My legs are not as long as yours, and it is a lot of hill."

"Of course. Sorry."

Once she's got her breath back, we continue, together still but slower, out of sync.

"Are you sure about this?" she asks, looking up the hill. "There is a reason we never walked Hangman's Hill. The memories up here, they are going to be ugly."

"I've seen ugly before."

"Seen people hanged?"

"No."

"I have."

"Ghosts at a castle or something?"

"Not ghosts." She hunches over, wraps her arms across her belly, but she keeps walking. "People. Two of them. Back home. Before..."

Before she came to England. Before she was even ten years old. That stops me dead. I knew that she'd seen some bad things, I've even heard her talk about a few of them, but that...

Poor Star. She's so bright, so exuberant, so woven into the fabric of Aldkey, I forget that she comes from a land where the country bled. I keep failing her, like I failed Ben. Is this what I do to everyone in my life?

I start walking again and quickly catch up with her.

"Maybe we should turn back." She looks up the hill to where the gallows once was. "You do not want to see what I have seen."

"If you can live with it, then I can. For Ben."

She looks at me. "What if he is what we see? What if we feel him die?"

When she puts it like that, it sounds grotesque, but isn't that what I've been chasing? To witness my friend's death. To know how and above all why. To know whether he pushed himself too hard or whether this was done to him.

"We can help him find peace," I say. "Or vengeance."

Ghosts drift past us as we walk, visions of those who've walked this way before. The power of the land is flowing through me stronger than ever. There's something else too, though, something darker. Ben twisted the magic at Morley's Farm to preserve the broken memories, but someone has twisted it here for another purpose, one I don't understand yet. All I know is the prickling in my spine that grows more intense with each footstep.

Someone is standing on the top of the hill, silhouetted against the clear sky. I get that same prickling feeling when I look at them. I raise the camera and zoom in. I can see him just clearly enough to recognise the face of Steven Rackham and to make out the map in his hand, his finger sliding across the page. It's a pale imitation of walking a trail, but if your connection to the land is deep enough, sometimes the map can become the landscape, and few people are more connected here than the Rackhams.

I lower the camera without taking a photo. I don't want to preserve Rackham or any of his ilk: the aristocracy, the landlords, the investors, the people who'll claim half a county is theirs while they spend their days in a London town house or aboard some yacht in the Virgin Islands, who only swoop in to take their rent or set new rules or build new roads, without any care for or understanding of the people whose lives they're battering about. I want them to fade into the oblivion of amnesia, a mistake buried so deep we never think of it again. Rackham doesn't deserve to be part of this place or how people see it.

We round the corner of a broken shed that used to shelter livestock. Two men in hi vis jackets are standing around a theodolite, taking readings of the surrounding terrain.

"You work for him?" I ask, pointing up the hill.

One of the men frowns, looks where I'm pointing, then back at me.

"Not that it's any of your business," he says, "but yes, currently."

He's better spoken than I expected, probably a surveyor rather than a labourer. I know it's a symptom of my own class-based bullshit, but I can't help thinking that he ought to

know better than to work with Rackham. This guy is edu-
cated, informed, presumably intelligent, he should know
how important this landscape is, that it can't be replaced
once you trash it. There is no second chance.

But then, a surveyor's job isn't to protect the landscape.
It's to record it, to tame it, to trap it like a plant pressed
between the pages of a book. He's the wrong person to look
to for assistance. Right now, he's the enemy, helping Rackham to reinforce his borders, to cut the land into pieces for
him and his friends to control.

I stride past and the beat of my feet against the ground
becomes a heartbeat, becomes a drumbeat, the terrible per-
cussion accompanying a doomed man to the gallows. I know
the condemned walked this way, and there's a trace of their
dread trailing up the hill. I see one of them out of the corner
of my eye, a man whose head hangs as heavy as his chains.
The surveyor shivers at the touch of something he can't
see and the theodolite falls from his hand to crack against a
stone.

Then I step through a gate into the next field and that
echo of the death march vanishes. Paths have power, but so
do boundaries, and this one has broken the flow of memory
up the hill. I pick out the rhythm of the world again, but the
ghost of a doomed man is gone.

The surveyor's phone rings and he answers.

"Yes, of course Mr Rackham." He signals to his assistant,
who picks up the theodolite. "We're going to move down the
hill, carry on there."

The wind hits, cold and sudden. I feel like something is
being stripped away from me. I'm in a place of power, but
I've had to leave behind a part of what I brought. It's an
uphill struggle to keep the rhythm that gives me strength.
Was this what Ben walked into?

Star slows, shoulders tight, feet dragging.

"I am not sure this is a good idea," she whispers. "He owns
this land."

"I didn't think you cared about trespass."

"Not like that. Feel the magic."

She's right. The land is responding to Rackham. The power that was flowing to me like an old friend now runs back to him like a whipped dog, too scarred and scared to disobey.

That fear is in Star's voice too. She's faced terrible people before and this hill is a chilling reminder of them. Now Rackham stands in their place, as arrogant, as dominant, as cruel. Those experiences gave her a strength of character I can barely dream of, but they gave her vulnerabilities too, places where the least pressure draws a gasp of anguish. I should give her what she wants, grant her the grace of permission to leave. That's what I should do for a friend. But this is about Ben. What the two of us had went beyond friendship and I need Star's help to see it through.

My power is waning despite the strength of my strides. I need something to focus me. I think of Ben, ascending this hill a few days before. I remember how we used to walk together. I seek out that pace.

Ben appears beside me. He's walking this path, an old right of way that Rackham has deliberately left to grow over. The landlord is trying to wipe it off the maps, to remove anyone else's right to be here. Ben walks with power and focus, each footstep slamming into the ground, a reminder that a way is worn by the thousands of people passing along it. As he reinforces a route older than any of us, he summons its strength.

Star trails behind as I match steps with Ben. The two of us walk together, steps perfectly attuned. I can feel his anger at what Rackham's doing and a deep determination to fix it. There's a raw, wounded feeling underneath, something that Ben himself can't acknowledge. I don't want to see it either, don't dare find out how far my friend had slipped into his misery. It's not what I need now. It's not how this magic is powered.

148

ANDREW KNIGHTON

Drawing on Ben's feelings makes me stronger. The land and I find our connection. The power of centuries flows through me and I glimpse ghosts in the clothes of late Victorian respectability, ambitious workers and sober clerks, housewives and housemaids; walking groups from the age of the great battles for access to the land. Ramblers reinforcing this path with every step, reminding the landowner that there are rights deeper and more ancient than his. These people have been threatened, bullied, chased off by rich men across the county, wherever there's a place worth walking. They keep going anyway and now they walk together. A single cotton spinner from the factories makes a thread so slender it would snap at the slightest tug. A thousand make a cord so strong it can hold a land together.

I'm not prone to patriotism, but this is the England I believe in. It's rooted in dirt and endurance, in shared struggle, not the solitary swagger of the people who appear in oil paintings. It's the nation that I come from. It gives me strength.

Those spirits fall away and others rise around me. These are chanting their defiance, waving fists and walking sticks and banners. It's so long since I've been part of a protest, I'd almost forgotten how it felt, a power that will raise you up and drag you along, that gives you confidence as long as you're on the same course as the people around you. Though I can't see them, I know that the landlord's thugs are waiting on the hilltop for these protesters, just like Rackham is waiting for me. Was he waiting for Ben too? I glance at Ben's ghost and I can't tell who his anger is pointed at, but I can feel it burning bright.

Star gasps. Though it's not loud, that one real sound cuts through the echoing roar and a centuries-old crowd fades away. She's fallen behind by twenty feet as her stop-start walk hooks another thread, so I match her pace to see it, find myself facing jailers with heavy sticks and a crowd soaked in cruelty. They cry out, baying for the end of a life.

"Come on." I hold out my hand. "You've got this."

"She is innocent." Star reaches for a woman trudging up the hill, head bowed, hands shackled. "She is innocent and they are going to kill her. I can not go there. I can not see that."

"We're going for Ben."

I drag myself away from his side and back towards Star. In any other place, I would lose the ghosts and the thread of power they've given me, but my connection with Ben keeps the memories flowing, voices whispering at the edge of silence, the ground thrumming with a buried strength. Will this path endure? Will the land be ours to walk or the Rackhams' to contain?

I take Star's hand, draw her forward one trembling step after another. I lend her my will.

"You can do this," I insist, and Star lets me sweep her along, blue hair hanging past her mirrored glasses.

A hedgerow looms ahead of us and a metal bar gate through it. Someone has tried to chain the gate shut, but the chain has been broken and rusted links trail in the dirt. The gate has sagged into that dirt too, when it was mud in the winter, and now it's baked in place by the packed, dry ground, cold metal barring our path. Beyond it lies the final field, rolling down from the peak of the hill.

I grab the top of the gate and my boots clang against steel as I climb. At the top I stop, detached from the ground, feeling the powers at play. This is a field boundary, reinforced by centuries of law and expectation, by the ritual observances of ownership. But I follow a path, worn into the ground by generations of travellers. Two threads of power cross here, fighting to control the landscape.

Now I sense what I'm in for. The running stitch of pathways against the slashing blade of boundaries. Me and Star against that lone figure silhouetted against the sky.

Ben's ghost pauses beside me on the gate, taking a deep breath, bracing himself. He raises a hand, almost touches his eyebrow, then lowers his hand in a clenched fist. This is what he came for, to fight the eternal battle of England for the sake of a single small village. His whole adult life, he's battered his head against the pillar of national politics, and all he's got from it is pain. The roads are still clogged with cars, the halls of power with corruption, and men like Rackham get richer while others get thrown out of their homes. But if he can win this one struggle, if he can make things right in the place he was born, then he can prove that victory is possible, that the battle is worth the pain. And if he can't...

His mind slides off that thought, back into the certainty of his cause. Sitting beside me, he blazes with a power so bright and beautiful it makes me want to weep. It's the righteousness that drove him throughout his life and that drove me away, embodied in the power of the land. It's the certainty I need, the moment of knowing what the world is and why it matters.

He burns brightly, but that doesn't mean he had to burn out. He was pushed to this point by the people who make no space for others, who want it all for themselves. I'll show them. I'll make it right. I'll finish his work.

With one hand, Star grips the top bar of the gate, swallows, braces herself. What does she see on Hangman's Hill? The ghosts going to the gallows? The coffins carried away? The terrible moment in between, when a single step leads from life into death?

I lay my hand on her shoulder.

"You don't have to come, Star. I can do this. I understand now."

She steps away, opens her backpack, pulls out a can of brown spray paint. It rattles as she shakes it, hisses like a snake as she paints a message across the grass and dirt. It's childishly simple in design, will soon be worn and washed away, but that doesn't stop it existing as art. It's a game of hangman painted on the side of the hill, a half-made stick figure dangling from the gallows and three dashes beside him, ready for the letters to be guessed. She pulls out another can, red this time. Rattle. Hiss. Hiss. Three letters, the last with excess paint streaming from its end like blood from an open wound:

B E N

She puts the cans back into her pack, zips it forcefully shut, then grips the top of the gate with both hands. Ben's ghost hops down ahead of us, and together, we climb into the final field.

Chapter Eight

Steven Rackham is standing at the top of the hill, looking down at us with a smug sneer. He wears green Wellington boots, a three-piece tweed suit, and a striped tie in his old school colours, held in place with a pin in the shape of a shield. Designer sunglasses hide his eyes. It's the sort of outfit that looks perfectly normal in certain very specific, very wealthy circles. His house, a mansion with its own walled grounds, is only five miles away, but he lives on a completely different planet from the rest of us.

"This is my land." Rackham taps his map with a pencil.

"This is a public footpath," I reply.

Both statements are simultaneously true, both loaded with legal and social power. In this country, they coexist, even support each other if you squint at them in the light of tradition's setting sun. It's the intentions behind them that are incompatible.

Rackham runs his pencil carefully along the map and a figure appears briefly behind him, an eighteenth century Rackham proudly surveying the land, basking in his control. As the pencil stops the ghost fades, but his spirit lingers-- power, pride, disdain.

I remember another ghost, the memory of this modern Rackham chasing Ben and throwing stones. The man I'm facing has surely changed since then, but nothing I've seen or heard makes me think he's any kinder.

"You're not just here as ramblers." Rackham surveys me and Star, looks straight at the ghost of Ben, and sniffs dismissively. "Two intrusions in as many weeks."

"Is it an intrusion if the land welcomes us?" I ask, feeling its power through my feet.

"It's dirt, not a puppy."

"It's alive, and it remembers. I think you know that."

Above the mirrored sheen of his sunglasses, Rackham's brow furrows.

"I have work to do, and you have no business getting in my way."

"I have a right to be here."

"Well, you shouldn't." His pencil taps against the map again. "My family poured blood and sweat and money into this land, and we shouldn't have to tolerate randoms tramping across it, getting up to God knows what."

His words are calm, disdainful, the voice of a man who knows he will get what he's after. They make my heart hammer with fury.

"Other people's blood," I say. "Other people's sweat. Money earned off other people's work."

"Oh, so you're one of those." His tone is growing sharper. "Would you let some mud-stained stranger march through your living room?"

"I haven't fenced off half the county and called it my house."

"There it is," he sneers. "Jealousy. Everyone wants to steal a piece of my land."

"The land belongs to all of us."

"All of you?" He laughs derisively. "None of you know how to take care of it."

"You call this taking care?" My tone sharpens too, our voices slashing like knives. "Building concrete monstrosities on ancient meadows? Driving out families that have lived here their whole lives?"

"Families who don't appreciate what this place is really worth. You're like little children, grasping for pearls because you want to play at marbles."

"So we should let you take it from us?"

"Take it from you?" His laughter becomes a snarl. "When my father died, we almost lost the house. Grasping little oiks with their inheritance taxes, trying to take my home from me."

"You're mad because someone asked you to share your mansion?"

"My home, where I grew up, where my mother was lying in bed, catatonic with grief. And they wanted to turf her out? Fuck them. I beat them and their lawyers, and I'll beat anyone who tries to take what's mine again."

There's a humanity here that catches me by surprise, a sadness seeping out through the indignation. But there's a difference between understanding someone, even pitying them, and thinking they're right. I've seen farming communities collapse in neglect, homeless people living on the city streets. I've come here weighed down with the pain of my own grief. I have no patience for this level of ignorance and arrogance, this brittle husk where empathy for his fellow humans should be.

"You were here when Ben died." I walk right up to Rackham and the ghosts emerge with my footsteps; ramblers and protesters alongside me and Star, executioners and their victims around Rackham. When I stop, the darkest figures take the longest to fade, marking the boundary between life and death, power and poverty, that played out on Hangman's Hill.

I clench my fists. This man wanted to destroy all that remains of Multhorpe. He set his magic against Ben's for the sake of control.

"If I'd been here, I would have sent that little blighter packing," he says. "Instead, he wrecked the work I've done, the memories I've bound. I've had to send surveyors across half the county to remind the land who's in charge."

"You killed my friend," I growl.

"He killed himself," Rackham snaps. He takes off the sunglasses, revealing flint grey eyes. "I just left the noose here."

I want to punch his smug face, but then he could call the police, get me dragged away for assault. You don't fight magic with fists.

The ghost of Ben walks past me, up the hill. Instead of following the trail, he steps off, starts a winding route around the hilltop. He's binding together memories of this place, all those people down the centuries. So many variations on the path that remains. He's tying it to the route that he's walked, the one that runs from Aldkey to Multhorpe and on, drawing together the strength of the land to resist Rackham. Surely this isn't the act of a man who wants to die.

We watch him. Tears sparkle at the corners of Star's eyes as she sees her friend perform a walk so erratic and irregular, so abstract and purposeless, it could be one of her works of performance art. Rackham watches with wry amusement, laughing when Ben stoops and slows, worn down by the strain of this power. For me, it's a lesson, a guide. I rejected Ben's path through the world once, railing against the intensity of it. Now I'm memorising every last footstep because when his ghost is done this will be my path to walk, to finish the work he began.

Ben's steps take him in a stuttering spiral around the top of the hill, tighter circles bringing him toward the peak. A look of pain crosses his face. He stumbles. I flinch, then brace myself as I realise that these are his final moments. Ben's face is anguished, but as long as I stand here staring his mind is hidden to me.

Doubt cracks the armour around my heart and Theresa's words creep in. "That boy had been looking for a way out of this cold, hard world since the day he was born." I set out to learn the truth, but the closer I've come, the more I've pushed it away. I want to believe this was an accident, a noble sacrifice, Ben pushing himself too far because he still hoped to succeed. But what if he did it on purpose, to escape his growing isolation and his unending fear of failure? What if the higher cause was just an excuse? Is it my fault then, for giving up on him?

I don't want to know, but I have to find out. That need draws me forward, seeking to match Ben's footsteps, to know his thoughts. But before I can get close, Rackham reaches out with the toe of his boot, draws a swift slash in the dirt of the path, and the memory is severed. Ben vanishes from view.

I jerk to a halt and stare at Rackham open-mouthed.

"Shame," he says with a grin. "Now you won't get to see the end."

"You can't do that." I point at the ground, a sharp, stabbing gesture. "He's part of this path. He's part of its power."

"I draw the boundaries here, and they're strong enough to hide your friend's last moments." He licks his lips. "Unless you want to make a deal, of course. I could let you see what happened to him, but then you have to leave. No more messing with my land, from you or any of your strange little walkers' coven. Multhorpe is mine."

I look at Star, who looks back at me uncertainly. We came all this way for Ben. We both need to know. Besides, Theresa rejected Ben's way just as much as Rackham's. Who's to say we'd be doing the right thing if we complete his magic here?

Ben, that's who. He wouldn't have done this if it wasn't going to protect the people who lack power to protect themselves.

I run a hand through my hair, look left and right, trying to remember where Ben began his spiralling path. It's hard to tell on a blank green hillside.

"You wouldn't be bargaining if you knew you could beat us," I say.

"So what, you're going to summon up your power and fight me?" Rackham laughs. "Fireballs at dawn like some storybook wizard?"

"I'm going to walk his path." I take a few steps where I think I need to be and the ghost of Ben reappears, leading the way.

"What good will that do you, hm?"

I don't answer. I don't need to. My walk will build its own momentum, will bind me to the ghost of Ben. Rackham won't be able to keep me from completing the work Ben began. I'll heal this place and I'll see the truth.

For better or for worse, I'll know.

But Rackham's set on resisting. He flicks his map open, pulls out a pencil, starts reinforcing lines, boundaries as they are or as they could be; a landscape sliced apart and constrained, life squeezed into the shrinking spaces where authority lets others live. The power starts to fade from the path beneath my feet.

I'm not letting people like this win, so I start walking, drawing that power back through the ground, reinforcing it. As I follow the pattern Ben showed me, he reappears at my side. We fall into step and I start to see the memories he summoned up.

A woman walks with us for a moment on her way to the gallows, filled with horror and dread. I walk slowly, feet dragging, sinking into her rhythm. This is her end, and it will be mine too if I'm not careful. She's one of us, and it's important that she's remembered, but we'll lose if we let ourselves be defined by those in control.

Ben leads me as I pick up my pace, leaving the woman behind for brighter memories. A couple ambling across the hillside hand in hand. A few of the ramblers I saw earlier, enjoying the view from upon high. They show me where they walked, what this land meant to them, and then they fade away.

Not everyone is welcoming. As I turn the confident strides of ramblers into the march of protesters, thugs appear and block the way, paid muscle sent to stop people enjoying their rights. I, Ben, and the woman between us clench our fists in unison, bracing for a confrontation. The people around us have worked long weeks in the factories, fed the industrial machine that is England, and they've earned their chance to walk on its green and pleasant land.

The power of the moment tries to sweep me along, but I resist, let those ghosts go, and force myself to a slower, more hesitant pace, just like Ben has done. A stone-age hunter appears, and we connect his memory to that of the marchers through a grim thread of determination. Then we pass from him to a pair of medieval children, sharing his fear of the monsters lurking in a harsh winter. Every change of pace or direction is a step across memory, and now I understand what Ben was doing: binding them together, strengthening the threads of this path through the past, making it so strong it can never be severed. It's a magic of belonging, of showing how every person passing through is part of this place. But the power it takes to reinforce those connections drains me, just like it drained Ben. He stumbles, rights himself, keeps walking, and I follow, trembling, in his wake.

We continue in a spiral around the hill, slipping from one moment to the next, threading them together. At the top stands Rackham, phone in hand, making calls to lawyers and bankers, reinforcing the power of wealth, of division, of boundary. It clenches around us, closing off paths we could have taken. Ben's image grows faint, fades from view, and my chest tightens. I alter my path, shorten and lengthen my stride, desperately looking for the friend I've already lost twice, who I can't bear to lose again. My heart races and my fingers tremble. Sweat runs down my face as I strain to find the path, to find the pace, to find him.

Then Ben shimmers back into sight. That should reassure me, but instead it drenches me in dread. He's pale, face scrunched, wobbling as he walks, and I realise that he's feeling the same things I am; the strain and the pain of trying to hold threads of memory together, the fear of failure. My pulse races and I clutch my chest as every nerve in my body tingles.

I understand now. I have to do this.

Then there's a hand in mine, not the hand of a ghost but that of a living, breathing friend.

"What can I do?" Star asks, looking at me with concern.

"This," I say, squeezing her hand, feeling her strength restoring mine. It's not a power that I'm taking from her, but one created by our connection. I've been trying to bind the ghosts together single-handed, but you can't build belonging on your own.

A man in chains appears in time with our footsteps, then speeds up as bullets whip past him, a prisoner on the run. We run with him, Star howling with laughter, until the ghost disappears. It doesn't matter that we can't see his fate--an act of defiance is still a victory.

"I am going to paint the fuck out of that," Star declares, then she points on around the hillside. "Look."

There's Ben again, and past him Rackham, watching us with mounting tension, his back stiff, the map twisting between his fingers.

We're nearly at the top now, Ben and Star and I, nearly to the place where Ben's story ends. Death dwells on Hangman's Hill, where feet jerked their last steps at the end of a noose. I'd understand if Star didn't want to come closer, but she walks with me, following Ben's trail, keeping his pace.

Ben's weakening and so is his ghostly body, its trace becoming fainter. This is the point where he faltered, where the struggle became too much. He'd spent his strength without binding the last of the threads and his work unravelled when he died. But Star and I are together. We can do this.

I dig deep into the land, press at it with my feet, find its strength. I don't call on other ghosts any more. The final memory is different now from when Ben walked this way. I don't see what he saw; instead I see him, lonely and exhausted, giving the land the last of his power as he staggers to the top of the hill. There, he sinks to his knees, clutching his chest.

There are tears in my eyes as I approach Ben. He's not walking now, but one hand pounds the ground, keeping up a rhythm, desperately trying to finish the magic he began. His eyes shine. He's smiling. He thinks that he's won, and that breaks my heart all over again.

It hurts to come closer, knowing what's about to happen, but I have to know what he's feeling. I have to know, did he want to die here, the martyr, the suicide; or was he just too stubborn to surrender? This is one memory I won't fight off, won't break through. It's a memory I crave.

Why can't I feel what he feels?

Star is trying to get my attention. I have to ignore her, to focus on Ben, to match his pace and hear his heart. I kneel beside him and beat my fist against the ground, joining his rhythm once more. My pulse is racing, skinny clammy, body trembling. I'm so close.

I look at Ben and match the rhythm he's making with that last desperate beating of his fist. He's the heart of a tangle of memories we've bound, the place where I will become history. If I lean in, I'll feel his thoughts, I'll know the truth. I dread that answer as much as I need it, but this is our last shot at reconciliation, my last chance to show him that I care.

I raise my fist, ready to beat out that rhythm one last time.

I raise my eyes and look out across the land.

From here, I can see all the way to the sea, that dark and formless place where there are no paths, no memories, where solid ground is replaced by the constantly shifting waves. That sight holds me in its vastness and I take a deep breath, contemplating the untethered realm to which we return.

I unclench my fist and stand. As Ben's ghost falls, I pick up his rhythm with my feet. I stride along the path, abandoning his memory, his truth, but carrying the power of this place. The path is blurred by my tears and by a thousand ghostly memories. Spirits of every era walk together down the hill, along a path where we all belong. They cascade through the hedge with no regard for the border it represents, treading out the path to Multhorpe, to Aldkey, to the world. Together, we form a new thread. A new magic. A stitch that binds and heals.

Rackham stands in the middle of the path. His face is red, his teeth bared.

"You think you've won?" he snarls. "That this will stop everything I have planned?"

I don't know. I'm not Ben. I have no idea whether this magic is powerful enough to change the minds of planners, to strengthen the hearts of protesters, to comfort a fractured community. Ben believed in it, and though he knew better than me, I don't know how well he was grounded in reality come the end. I'll never know.

When I look back, he's not on the hill any more. I let out a breath I've been holding for years and turn my face west towards Aldkey. Towards home.

Chapter Nine

The weight of the coffin on my shoulder feels wrong, too light to be the weight of a whole life and yet too heavy to bear. We carry that burden between us: me, Star, Lynn, some professionals from the funeral home. We make a solemn procession, slow steps all in sync, carrying Ben carefully up the steps to the church, through that arch of medieval stone, down the nave, watched by friends and family, comrades and colleagues, all the people whose lives Ben touched. So many of them. He fought hard, changed many lives for the better, though his own was far too short.

So many others have walked this way down the centuries, engraving their grief into the stones, and our steps evoke them. We share a dreadful solidarity, and that connection helps me to endure, but I don't look at them, don't open myself to their thoughts. Today, I have enough memories of my own.

We lay Ben down in front of the altar and take our seats. I fight the urge to loosen my collar. It's so long since I've worn a suit. These things are ridiculous, but I'm not wearing it for me. It's a mark of respect, for Ben's parents.

Cerys leads the service. I couldn't do that in her shoes, but she's always wielded a terrible strength. Grief is kept for her garden, where she can pace alone and unseen; here, she has another duty to fulfil. From her place in the pulpit, she delivers a sermon and a reading, then leads us all in hymns. The words wash over me. I want to be respectful to her faith but none of it feels relevant. All that matters is the coffin, sitting at the head of the church, a wreath of white flowers lying on the lid.

Ben's body is still in there. That's a crazy thought. His feet will never walk those paths again, but they're lying in that coffin, here with us now. I almost laugh at the absurdity of the thought, almost cry as I choke it back. Star rests a hand on my shoulder and we lean into each other, looking for comfort.

There are so many ghosts in this church, engraved into stone by centuries of the most powerful emotions--the joy of marriage, the grief of loss, the rapture of faith. We used to draw them out, back when we were first learning. If I wanted to, I could take a few steps now and see a teenage Ben, grin wide as he discovered his powers. But even when the service is over, when we pick the coffin up and carry it out to the graveyard, I don't seek that connection with the land, don't look for the memories. Today isn't for clinging to the past.

There are trees around the edges of the graveyard, flowers growing beside some of the graves. New life for old. That's something Ben would have wanted.

Cerys is saying something again as they lower Ben into the ground. This time her voice cracks. As Dom takes her hand, she starts to cry, and he pulls her close. He looks at me with a sad smile and I take some small comfort in knowing that I did something good while I was back in town.

When all the ceremonial parts are done, mourners mill around in the graveyard. There are photographs and food waiting in the church hall; the problem is that no one wants to be the first to leave this frozen moment, to let go of Ben. But I've done that already, or started to at least, up on Hangman's Hill. I can lead the way now.

I walk over to Cerys and Dom. Star follows me.

"I'm going for a walk," I say. "To clear my head."

"I understand," Dom says softly.

Cerys nods stiffly. She wants me to go to the church hall, I'm sure, to do things the proper way, but really, she'll be happier if I'm not there.

"What will you do after this?" she asks. "Are you staying in town?"

"For a little while. I'm researching a book on local walks, and then I'll need to write it up. I thought I might rent a flat here for a few months, maybe carry on Ben's work at Multhorpe."

"That would be good." She frowns, wipes away a tear. "I'd like to help, if that's all right."

"Of course."

Action will suit her more than me, as a way of healing, but it'll be good for both of us. I can't heal the rift with Ben, but perhaps I can bridge the chasm between me and his mother.

Theresa's at the gate of the graveyard with some others from Multhorpe. She stops me and Star as we pass.

"You did something," she says accusingly.

"We tried," is all I'll admit.

"The stoppage on the road construction, that was you."

I shake my head. "That was Ben."

"And the new issues with the planning application?"

I bob my head from side to side. That one might be me. These things are complicated, but a lot of local councillors like to go out walking, and that's a good time for the land to speak to them, to remind them what beautiful country this is, what a shame it would be to let it be despoiled.

"We should talk," she says. "There's a meeting coming up."

"I know." I pull a crumpled leaflet from my pocket. Not much of an apology, but there will be time to say sorry later. "I'll be there."

"We'll be there," Star says. "Art activism, man, it's the way to get young people engaged."

Theresa looks sceptical, but she's got what she wanted, so she lets us pass.

We step through the graveyard gate into the street and I feel as though a trance is lifting, like I'm connecting to a reality I've been watching from a thousand miles away. A car rumbles past. Two teenagers throw chips at each other.

"Wait a moment." Star disappears around a corner, reappears with a backpack that sloshes and clinks. "I figured we would need supplies. Where are we going?"

"Cliffs," I say, unfastening my top button and loosening my tie.

"Of course." Star shoulders her bag and we walk.

There's a back way to the cliffs above town, a less trodden path for those in the know. After a couple of side streets and a building site, we reach a pasture that brings back happy memories.

"We were so young then," I say, as we walk past the indifferent sheep.

"We are not so old now," Star says. "Got our whole lives ahead of us." She cringes immediately. "Did I just say that?"

"He'd understand." I watch gulls sweep past overhead. "And it's true."

We settle into a familiar rhythm and a memory emerges from the earth. Three teenagers walking across the field, sharing a single bottle of cider and a handful of dirty jokes, thinking that they're so very grown up. Me, Star, Ben. Young and glorious.

I watch the ghost of Ben, seeking some sign that can't possibly be there. He's a memory; nothing that's happened this week will change him. He can't forgive me because as far as he knows we haven't even argued.

The closer we get to the cliffs, the more memories arise, a dozen different versions of ourselves, maybe more; different ages, different clothes, different conversations. The repetition of those same three figures makes it cruelly obvious that only two of us remain.

I wipe away tears. "I've got to stop doing this to myself, calling him up like this. I've got to let it go."

"The memories are not what you must let go." Star taps her chest. "The memories make you, they drive you. It is the grief you have to release."

"Fuck." I shake my head. "When did you get so wise?"

"While you were away, of course."

We stop near the top of the cliff and sit down next to the strip of dirt that passes for a path. Beyond the cliff edge, the sea fills our world to the horizon, sunlight shining off its merciless roil. Star opens her bag, takes out two bottles of beer, opens them and hands one to me.

"To Ben," she says, raising her bottle in a toast. "It was good that you made that last walk for him."

"I thought that was what I was doing, but..." I take a sip of the beer. It refreshes me more than I deserve. "You can't make peace with the dead. I was just trying to make myself feel better about how I treated him."

"How you treated each other." She looks out across the sea, perhaps to a country she's never been back to. "You are still alive, Paul. There is nothing wrong with looking after yourself. Maybe that is what Ben needed to learn."

"I was marking my territory, shouting at the world about how I knew him first, how I loved him best. Protecting myself from the consequences of my own--"

"Oh, will you shut up!" The vehemence in her voice catches me by surprise. I stare at her and she stares right back. "What?"

"I don't..."

"You are doing it again, building a wall of words. You need to let go, to move on."

"How can I? We still don't know why he..."

I can't say it. Not here, surrounded by the happy memories, by a dozen younger versions of him.

For the first time, I realise that I'm jealous of Steven Rackham. Not because of his wealth, his power, his land. Because he has certainty. He knows how the world is meant to be, with him at the top and everybody else in their place, with fixed rules and authority. That certainty is one more border, one more barrier sealing off his territory, separating him from the rest of the world. We've both been trying to lay claim to something we felt entitled to, whether it was land or the memory of a lost friend. But those things aren't ours. When we try to contain them, it's ourselves we close off.

I don't want to be separate from the world. I want to live in it. I want to change it, like Ben did.

I take off my shoes and socks, press my toes into the grass, into the dirt beneath. Star grins and does the same. She has a good eye for a moment, whether it's of profundity or of fun, and she'll happily go along with either.

I down the rest of my beer, hold my hand out for another, which Star graciously provides. Then we stand up, cross the path, and keep walking. There's nothing between our feet and the land, no barriers to protect us from the memories it holds, whatever power and danger lurks within. The feeling of exposure is a terrifying jolt through my chest that fades into a moment of peace.

A single memory comes with us: the ghost of Ben, ten years ago, spinning as he staggers, half drunk, towards the cliff edge. Lying back on the grass, younger versions of me and Star shriek in laughter and alarm.

"What?" Ben calls out. "You're never going to take a risk? Never going to push at the world to see if it'll push back?" He flings his arms into the air. "Come on world, push me!"

I lean in and kiss his ghost on the cheek. Then I let the power go, let the vision of him scatter into motes of light that glitter on the sea and disappear into fathomless darkness.

# # # # #

ROZ CLARKE & JOANNE HALL

ACKNOWLEDGEMENTS

Teresa Nielsen Hayden once mentioned, on *Making Light*, that Mormon teens are sent on their proselytizing missions without enough food money. The goal is not for them to convert anyone, but to discover that the outside world is full of slammed doors and hungry nights. Ever since then, my household (very queer, interfaith Jewish and Neopagan) has invited clean-cut young door-knockers in for dinner whenever we get the chance. This book owes a good deal to Teresa, and to those wide-eyed young men trying to politely figure out who's married to whom.

It also owes a lot to that household: many thanks to Sarah, Jamie, Shelby, Nora, Lemur, Cordelia, and Marius for not only making sure I have writing time, but for pressing food on visitors, scrambling to find resources for panicked strangers, and inviting local candidates to argue about affordable housing in the shade of our porch. I love you all, even and especially when we're stretching that porch across an ocean.

—*Ruthanna Emrys*

Walking a Wounded Land wouldn't exist without Rebecca Solnit's book *Wanderlust*, which provided much of the inspiration. Thanks to Al Macleod, Adi Waite, Caro Childs, Cathryn Rose, Dion Winton-Polak, Mavis Cruet, Sue Ainslie, Lynda Boothroyd, Francesca Barbini and Milena Buchs for providing feedback on earlier drafts. Huge thanks to Roz, Jo, and Cheryl for seeing the story to publication.

And as always, my biggest thanks to Milena for all the support, encouragement, and long walks.

—Andrew Knighton

ROZ CLARKE & JOANNE HALL

ABOUT THE AUTHORS
AND EDITORS

Ruthanna Emrys is the author of *A Half-Built Garden*, *Winter Tide*, and *Deep Roots*, as well as co-writer of Reactor's Reading the Weird column with Anne M. Pillsworth. She writes radically hopeful short stories about religion and aliens and psycholinguistics. She lives in a labyrinthine apartment in the Netherlands with her wife and their large, strange family. There she creates real versions of imaginary foods, gives unsolicited advice, and occasionally attempts to save the world.

Growing up, Andrew Knighton's goal was to go on fantastical adventures in impossible worlds. When that didn't work out, he started imagining the adventures instead, and a writer was born. He's now the author of the Forged For Destiny trilogy and the Executioner series, as well as assorted short stories, comics, novellas, and murder mystery games. He lives in Yorkshire with an academic and a cat, growing vegetables and striving for a brighter future, while still hoping that a magical portal will open between the broad beans. You can find more of him at andrewknighton.com.

Roz Clarke likes to play around with words; her own and other people's. She has short stories in several anthologies, edits novels for Kristell Ink, and is best known for her editing partnership with Joanne Hall, which has produced such anthologies as *Airship Shape & Bristol Fashion* and the BSFA award-nominated *Fight Like A Girl*. You can twt her at @zora_db, or skeet @rozc.bsky.social.

Jo Hall was formerly Acquisitions Editor at Grimbold Books and loves working with authors to help them unleash their visions on the world (for good or ill). Her novels have previously been shortlisted for the Tiptree, Lambda and British Fantasy awards. She can be found on Bluesky @ hierath77.bsky.com.

Roz and Jo have been working together since the Bristol F&SF group started running BristolCon, brainchild of the late Colin Harvey, of which Jo was Chair and Roz held various roles on the concom. Both writers and editors in their own right, they first collaborated on *Colinthology*, a memorial anthology for Colin. They now collaborate regularly on wrangling chickens and digging the vegetable beds on their smallholding in South Wales, with their housemate Heather, Jo's partner Chris, and a motley collection of dogs and paperbacks. You can follow their blog on forest gardening and regenerative living at meddwlcoed.wordpress.com.